FARE DEAL

Written and Published
by

Rising Brook Writers

DISCLAIMER:

SPECIAL THANKS:

*SCC's Your Library Team at the Rising Brook Branch
Pauline Walden for original artwork*

PUBLISHED BY: *Rising Brook Writers*
RBW is a voluntary charitable trust. RCN: 1117227
© Rising Brook Writers 2010
*The right of Rising Brook Writers to be identified as the
author of this work has been asserted in accordance with sections
77 & 78 of the Copyright Designs and Patents Act 1988*

First Edition

ISBN 978-0-9557086-7-1

*www.risingbrookwriters.org.uk
and on FACEBOOK and MySpace*

£5-00
Donation
Appreciated

*A project funded by the
Grassroots Grant initiative of the
Office of the Third Sector*

*Online and Library Workshop
Contributors:*

*Susan Cantrill
Kayley Day
Martin Haywood
Clive M Hewitt
Edith Holland
Yasmin Lewis
John Price
Stephanie M Spiers
Pauline Walden (artwork)
Elizabeth Whitehouse
A Christine Williams*

Acknowledgement

Rising Brook Writers are very grateful to Staffordshire Community Foundation for awarding this project a Grassroots Grant to support the charity's Online Outreach Programme.
'Fare Deal' is a jointly written farce put together by participants scattered from Cannock to Meir Heath, and from Great Haywood to Highfields, all joined via email and broadband internet connection.

This tale of mayhem was built up week by week by means of the charity's weekly email bulletin which is distributed to senior citizens scattered right across the entire Borough of Stafford. The writers' ages range between early 50s to nearly 90s.

If you can imagine pegging washing out on a line the principle is the same, or, perhaps, compiling a jig-saw when the picture on the box lid keeps changing. As contributors emailed in their pieces to the bulletin editor the jig-saw pieces of the story gradually came together in chunks of around 500 words; each piece being shuffled forwards and backwards to achieve the best fit. Farce is difficult even for professional writers but the absurdity of the unfolding catastrophe should stretch the chuckle muscles.

MONDAY

Monday with Biggles JP

'Bandit at two o'clock,' yelled Biggles. As the attacker came out of the sun, he scanned the space around him. All clear. Biggles wrestled with the controls to adjust his speed and manoeuvre his kite out of danger. Still the attacker was locked on to him. He braced himself for impact. Thud!

'Blood and stomach pills,' groaned Biggles.

Moments later he brought the taxi to a halt and began the essential checks. 'Tib., fib., spectacles, testicles. All present and correct.' Biggles tweaked his moustache. 'Another one you've walked away from, old son,' he muttered. 'Better take a shufti at the damage.'

Opening the door of his Vauxhall Vectra, Biggles unzipped his flying jacket and gave the bodywork the once over. On the passenger window there were spots of blood. Biggles walked back down the road and saw it lying there; a magnificent cock pheasant with traces of red in its nostrils. 'Ah,' said Biggles, 'dinner!'

He picked up the bird and put it in the boot.

'Control to Kilo-Bravo-Oscar,' barked the car radio. 'Come in Kilo-Bravo-Oscar ... Biggles! Where the chuffing hell are you? Over.'

'Kilo-Bravo-Oscar to Control. Come in, Wingco. Just stopped to help an old bird who looked a bit groggy. Over,' replied Biggles, applying the mushroom principle he always used when dealing with authority: keep 'em in the dark and add manure now and again.

'I hope you're not giving free rides. Anyway, I was on my mobile to Pat.' Surprise, surprise thought Biggles. 'She was on a break but I could hear their radio in the background. Hopalong's broken down again so get yourself over to the crematorium and pick up some ashes for a Mrs Richardson. Over.'

'Wilco, Wingco. Over and out,' said Biggles, wondering just how sweet his boss really was on the generously proportioned controller at Cavalry Cabs and how much it was just a ruse to nick business from them. He wouldn't be that devious, thought Biggles, would he?

Ten minutes later, with the urn safely in the boot, Biggles set off to return the late Mr Richardson to his nearest and dearest. As he pulled into the drive of the 1930s semi, the front door opened and a neat, little grey-haired figure stood on the step waiting for him.

'Hello, Mrs Richardson. D'you remember me? Bobby Owen. I used to come into your pet shop when I was a kid. What was it called? Dickeyfido's, wasn't it? Dickey – Mr Richardson – used to buy any baby rabbits I'd got.'

'Course I remember you, Bobby. It's just that you didn't have a moustache then.'

'Sorry to hear about Dickey. He was always good to me. Gave me a bit extra for the rabbits when I had to help Mum make ends meet after Dad left.'

'Yes, everyone liked Dickey,' said Mrs Richardson,

her voice breaking.

Bobby smiled at her. 'Well, he's back home now.'

'Oh, he was here yesterday. When I opened the curtains there was this wood pigeon in the tree. Of all the pets in the shop, Dickey loved birds the best. He even called me his Puddleduck. Said if there was anything in reincarnation, he'd come back as a bird. Bring him in, Bobby. I'll put the kettle on.'

Biggles opened the boot. 'Aaaah! What the chuffing hell?' He slammed the lid and wiped his eyes to get rid of whatever had hit him in the face. Moving to one side he slowly opened the boot again. The pheasant was standing by the upturned urn scratching away and sending what was left of old Dickey cascading out of the boot.

'Tea's ready, Bobby. Bring Dickey in. *Countdown*'s just starting. He never missed *Countdown*,' called Mrs Richardson from the hall. Shielding the boot best he could, Biggles grabbed the pheasant with one hand and tried to stuff as much as he could of Dickey back in the urn with the other.

'There you are you pesky rattlesnake!' Biggles turned. It was Hopalong, heading up the drive, fists clenched. 'Prepare to be separated from your breath.' Biggles shut the boot as Hopalong lunged at him. 'Give me that goddam urn,' Hopalong growled.

'Bring him in, Bobby. They're asking Carol Vorderman for two big ones from the top. That always tickled Dickie.' Hopalong wrestled the boot catch from Biggles but as the boot opened, Biggles shut it with his other hand. Open ... shut ... open ... shut, the boot lid gulped its way through the next five minutes until both men slumped on to the drive. Unhindered, the boot slowly opened and the pheasant flew into a nearby tree followed by an excited cry from the door-way, 'Dickey, Dickey. Come to Puddleduck.'

Late Sunday evening   EH

Late the previous evening Jim and Janice Jones, local Mayor and Mayoress, just back from one more official function were met in the hall by the ringing phone. Kicking off her shoes and with a weary sigh, Janice said, 'Yes'.

'You've got to do something quick,' came the ago-nised cry from Yvonne at the other end.

'Just a minute, hang on and let me get your Dad,' said her mother, 'Jim, Jim, come here and see what's the matter with our Yvonne. She sounds hysterical.'

'Oh, my goodness! What's gone wrong now?' he said as he came from the bedroom struggling to take off his jacket.

'Get me a drink, Jan. Sounds as if I shall need one. Now, sweetheart what's up? Calm down a bit and tell me.'

'Oh, Dad, the caterers have gone bust, that's what's up. I've been ringing you all evening. You've got to do something.' Jim could hear the panic rising but was, as non-plussed as she was.

'Where are you now love?' trying to calm her down he guessed where she was of course.

'I'm at Chummy's and his Dad heard it at the golf club. Why didn't you know as well?'

'That's no matter now,' muttered Jim. 'At this time

of night there's nothing to be done. Leave it to me, I'll sort it out in the morning.'

'But Chummy's Dad says the same thing and I shan't sleep a wink and it's only six days to the wedding,' and off she went in a flood of tears.

Her mother snatched the phone and as calmly as she could said, 'Just do as your Dad says for once. He'll sort it out in the morning,' and she collapsed in the armchair, knowing who would do the sorting out as usual. Even before going to bed she had made a list of phone calls for early Monday morning. Jim wasn't the only one who knew people.

Monday 07.30

Janice was on the phone to Cavalry Cabs. Wyatt Twerp happened to be her cousin and he owed her a favour for holding her tongue in his old lady's nasty divorce case.

'Hello, that you, Wyatt? I need a favour. Yes I know it's early in the day but it's urgent,' and she went on to explain why.

'You've got to juggle the bookings round for Saturday. It's an emergency. A wedding can't be put off that easy, so I need your help. Don't matter about the cost, we'll sort that out later. Think of the publicity that Jim can get for your football network, so just do it now.'

'Okay,' he said. 'Ring you back in ten minutes. There's an idea brewing,' and he cut her off.

Elsewhere on Monday morning CMH

Shouting into the garage as she passed, 'Put the kettle on, Hoppy. I'm as thirsty as a three-day camel on a five-day trip.' Pat stooped and gathered up the letters as she entered Cavalry Cabs' cramped office.

'Usual rubbish! I should tell Dai the Post to chuck the lot straight in the bin. Save me having to.' She looked at the outside of the letters and binned most, unopened.

'What's this? Trentby City Council Licensing Office. Now what's got up their combined jacksy?' A fast scan of the enclosures resulted in, 'Chuffing hell! Review of the vehicle operators' license and the suitability of drivers to ply for hire ... Heavens to Betsy! This means trouble with a capital Trub!'

Tea forgotten, she hurtled out of the office into the garage, just in time to meet Hopalong coming the other way with a tray of full tea cups. Out massing Hoppy and his tea tray, by at least twenty-five percent, Hoppy ended up having a tea bath on the floor.

'Get everybody together, Hoppy,' was her terse order. 'I don't care where they are; I want 'em here ... yesterday! We've got a few problems to sort out.' Turning on her heels she disappeared back into her cubby to phone her alter ego in Concorde Cabs.

For once the sound of Dusty's voice didn't have its usual sexually seething, but soothing, effect. 'Dusty, have you checked your post yet? Those ruddy sneaky council types are up to something! They're calling in all our licenses for review and that means medical checks, eye-sight checks, hearing checks, vehicle checks, police checks, paper work checks and all sorts of rhubarb. You remember what happened last time,' she wailed. 'I got dumped for being overweight and you got dumped, and fined, because you weren't wearing glasses! And it's only been six months since the annual check.'

'Slow down, Pat, my love. Slow down,' said Dusty soothingly. 'It's probably nothing to get excited about. Probably something to do with Trentby Weddings going bust and having to reassign the licenses. Dai hasn't been yet, he always takes his time going over the King Arthur bridge. He says he likes watching the river; but I've seen him. He's scared of heights and, let's face it, that bridge's none too solid looking. I'll call you when he's managed to get here. Love you!' He rang off, looked out of the window and saw Dai the Post half way over the bridge, standing frozen to the spot, tightly gripping the guard rails.

'Oh, ruddy hell. I suppose I'd better get the silly beggar off that bridge before he takes root.' Going onto the bridge he stopped alongside the postman. 'More fish in a butcher's shop than that river, Dai,' he said.

The sound of his voice worked to bring the pallid, fear-frozen, postman back to life. 'Yer, yer. I was just thinking how nice the river looked today. Nothin' 'bout fishin'. Had to give that up. The wife, you know?'

Once in possession of his mail Dusty, very carefully, read the letter in question. Then he passed it to Ace for a second opinion.

'Not a lot to go on there, Dusty,' said his second-in-command, and the most politically aware of the crew. 'There'll be the licenses vacated by the collapse of "Weddings" of course; and I know that old Jonesy wants more cabs on the road. You know, if we could get those limos, and drivers, from "Weddings" it'd be a step forwards for us.'

Dusty shook his head, 'Too much to hope for, Ace. The cash flow's dodgy and the reserves won't stand it. The bank manager has asked me to call in and discuss our account. I'm not expecting that to be cheerful. Maybe, depends on how much they're going for, we could get one or two but not the whole fleet.'

In the Cavalry Cabs office a similar conversation was taking place between Pat, Doc and Wyatt, but with a different outcome.

Monday morning across town   SMS

'I say, our Vera, I say.'

'What is it, Bertha? Can't it, wait? I'm still on the phone.' Vera clapped a gnarled hand over the mouth piece. 'It's him with the face. You know; can't raise the Titanic without a bit of poetry to help, get started.'

'Not the boy stood on the burning deck? Not him?'

'No ... no ... Charge of the light-brigade. Works wonders, a bit of Lord Tennyson; can raise the dead can our Alfred. But I've forgotten me top set of teeth which doesn't help so I had to play him a CD track of the reading. He said he liked the music.'

'What's he doing now?'

'He's gone to make a cup of tea, I think. He was a

bit shaken when the cannons went off in his digital hearing aid.'

'Put the phone down, Vera. I need a word in your ear, dear.'

'What's up? It's a bit early for a tea-break, it's only half-past-nine.' After patting the curls of a concrete perm, Vera turned up the volume in her own (NHS) hearing aid and gave her boss the full benefit of her one good eye.

Bertha was slumped onto the top end of the portacabin's homely working environment-cum-massage-parlour-client-waiting area's velvet-covered chaise longue and was teasing out a king-sized filter tip with a claw-length finger nail beautifully painted with the Union flag. Vera gazed hopefully at the silver cigarette case as it fell back into the vast depths of Bertha's silver-lamé handbag. Bertha never crashed the ash; she was good like that; she never encouraged her girls into bad habits.

'Trentby Discreet Escort and Phone-In Services are having a bit of a crisis.'

Vera said nothing. She had read the paper along with all the other girls. Actually she had read the paper to all the other girls because most of them didn't have English as their first language.

'That idiot Jim "flaming-hell-as-like" Jones has turned down my planning application.'

'What for Number 27?'

'Yes, for Number 27!'

'But he sold you the lease to Number 27... ' spluttered Vera, a hand automatically reaching out for the again-ringing phone. Her voice dropped three octaves and her vowels spread out like butter melting over hot crumpets: 'He-llo, Lady Vee, your Goddess of the Morning. How can I help you into paradise?' The voice returned to normal, 'Oh hello, Angie. It's you is it? Did you want to speak to Bertha?' Nodding in the affirmative, Vera handed over the mouthpiece and changed seats. 'She's in the pokey!'

'You what! You what! I'll flaming kill him. The rat,' bellowed the massage-parlour's generously proportioned proprietrix, her porcine countenance puce with rage and Buckingham Palace ear-rings swinging like chandeliers in a knocking shop as she banged down the phone. 'He's done it now! That ruddy swine. He's only gone and raided Angie's place.' Vera's toothless maw fell open in shock.

'Not Inspector Mackay from Vice? The rotten devil. He was only in here last night angling after a freebie with Olga.'

'There'll be no more freebies for the Vice Squad this week. Another fine and guess whose pocket it will be coming out of again.' The Madam grabbed a swing-backed leopard-skin jacket from the coat rack and put it on along with the striking blonde wig she kept handy for action on the severed head from a tailor's dummy by the answer machine. Easing out creases in a black satin mini skirt and checking her fish nets for any enlargements, she was ready for the off. Pausing only to squeeze her size nines into five-inch stilettos, Bertha wrenched open the door with stiffly-pointed fingers.

'Cheer up, luvvie. This Saturday's supposed to be a special occasion. Big hat. New frock. All the works … I love a wedding.'

'Yes, thank you, Vera. I hadn't forgotten.' Bertha stopped in mid-flight to consider. 'Derby match day. I'd better book some cabs in advance. Always a good night for us after Derby matches.'

Vera nodded: 'Consoling the losers and stroking the ego of the winners. Win-win.'

'That's what I like about you, Vera, good business head on those shoulders. But do try to find your top-set dear, you look like a face for radio this morning.'

The door banged shut leaving the pensioner to mind the business premises all on her own and once again the phone rang.

'He-llo, Lady Vee, your Goddess of the Morning. How can I help you into paradise?'

Monday at Concorde   CMH

The sexy throaty stage whisper of: 'Well, hello there, sexy,' coming through the control room's open hatch brought Dusty out of his reverie and his chair back onto four legs.

'Oh, flaming hell, Momma; I wish you wouldn't do that! You could give a fellow a heart attack.'

All fourteen stone of Momma Classidy shimmered into laughter as she said, 'I wish you could have seen your face just then. Day-dreaming about her were you?' She nodded towards the photo of Pat Walker, Dusty's opposite number from Cavalry Cabs, on top of the radio set.

'Yes, just a bit,' he admitted, which brought more laughter.

'More than just a bit my lad. More than that I'd say. Anyway, what have I got on the pick-up list?'

'Seventeen's out of the workshop and is yours for the day but there's nothing for the next half-hour, then the school runs start. I've got you and Ace pencilled in for the 'uphill' flights with Biggles and Ginger on the cross town stuff. Okay?'

'Roger, Wilco,' came the reply. 'With the blasted road works at the bridges again, we'll need to fly to be sure we get there in time.' A snort of disgust and she was gone.

The VIP phone rang. Picking it up he said, 'Concorde Cabs, Wingco speaking. How can I be of assistance?' The voice at the other end was one he knew well.

'Yes, Madam Mayoress, we can accommodate a wedding party on Saturday. Church of the Bleeding Heart ... midday. Flowers and red ribbons? No problem ... United football ground afterwards in time for the kick-off shouldn't be a problem. As long as the road works are finished anyway. But I'm sure that the Mayor can fix that ... Four cars to pick-up the bridal party at your address? Usual city account, is it?'

The phone went down and he swore, 'Red ribbons to the Clem Attlee, coals to Newcastle is that, old man Jones keeping the red flag flying for both the team and their party. Never miss a chance for self-advantage do councillors. Still it's all money in the bank; if I can get the city to pay up in time!'

The VIP phone rang again but before he could finish his usual speech another voice cut him off. 'Dusty, I want two cars on Saturday. Both to get to the Bleeding Heart by midday, one from here and one from Number 27.' It was Big Bertha his best customer, cash on the nail, clean fares, short runs, good tips, no problems.

He was stumped; all his cars would be in use but, with a bit of luck, he could chat to Pat and get her to swing a couple of cars in his direction. 'Not a great problem there, Bertha. Saturday, say 11.30 from Number 27 and 11.45 from your office. Is that okay?' It was. Now to chat to Pat.

The vicar   MH

He trudged down the road, his eyes firmly focused on the pavement. William Warmer, the plump vicar of the Church of the Bleeding Heart, hated Monday mornings but today was worse than usual, and it all stemmed from the appalling Sunday he'd had to endure.

He realised it was going to be a bad day when his nosy wife confronted him at breakfast with a half empty bottle of Jack Daniels and accused him of being a lush. He tried to explain it was for medicinal purposes only, but she didn't believe a word, and then to make matters worse she told him he could sleep on the couch until he gave up the booze.

At first he thought it would be nice to sleep alone and not have to listen to her constant snoring, however, it occurred to him that if he wasn't in the bedroom with his wife, there would be no role playing with fairy outfits and that would be a shame, because he had only recently found one big enough to wear.

On his arrival to take the usual Sunday morning

communion he had been disappointed to find less than twenty people in the church and, of those, fourteen were choir boys and girls, their conductor, an organist, a man who had come to his church every day for four years because someone had told him Elvis was going to return in the seat next to him, and Gwen, the cleaner, who had been cleaning the brass candle sticks continuously for two months and had caused a stir when his superiors wanted to know why he had purchased fifty bottles of brasso and fifty dusters out of petty cash.

Later in the day it had started to rain when he walked back to the church for evensong and he was pleasantly surprised to see a congregation of around forty sitting happily in front of him, along with the old dear in a wheelchair whose family left her in church while they went to the local to get legless.

So happily he sang all of the hymns with gusto and gave a rousing sermon and thanked them all for coming when he had finished. 'No, thank you, Vicar,' said a cheerful looking fellow at the back of the church.

'Sorry, I don't understand,' he replied cagily.

'Thank you for looking after my passengers. I told them to wait in the church when the coach broke down and it started to rain.'

'My pleasure, at least they were lucky enough to hear my rousing sermon, one of my best if I do say so myself.'

'I doubt it.'

'What do you mean?'

'Erm, I don't want to disappoint you too much,

Vicar, but they are all deaf and wouldn't have heard a word.'

William looked at the man and without saying a word he disappeared into the vestry and he didn't even have his fairy outfit to go home too.

When he arrived at the church vestry he was surprised to see the door was unlocked until he walked inside and found the cleaner still cleaning the candlesticks.

'Gwen, have you been home since yesterday?' he asked her.

'Oh yes, Vicar, I took the candlesticks home I hope you don't mind.'

'Don't you think you have cleaned the brasses for long enough? Look, they shine beautifully and to be honest when I took you on I meant for you to clean everything.'

'Sorry, I like to do a good job,' she replied, close to tears.

'I know you do, but I have an important wedding here on Saturday and the woodwork and the floor both need polishing.'

Instantly he said 'polishing' a glazed look came over Gwen and with a beaming smile she said. 'Polishing? Oh yes, I can do that. I think you ought to get some more furniture polish and dusters.'

He shook his head and made his way to his small office, and thought how he was going to explain the purchase of more polish and dusters.

Once there he sat down and sighed, before unlocking the bottom drawer of his desk to pull out a bottle of Jack Daniels and a crystal glass. He looked at the amber nectar and slowly pulled the cork and began to pour.

'Willie Warmer! What have I told you about drinking?'

He jumped up and managed to knock the glass off the desk and onto the floor where it smashed into little pieces. However, when he looked around he couldn't see his wife, so he warily opened the door and the only person he saw was Gwen singing an unrecognisable tune while she polished a pew.

He immediately sat back down and retrieved another glass from his drawer and poured a tot with a shaking hand.

'Got you there, didn't I?' said a gleeful voice.

'Who is that?'

'Don't you recognise my voice, Willie boy?'

'Should I? Where are you?'

'Oh, sorry. I am not used to this yet. Hold on a sec.'

William looked around and wondered if someone was playing games with him.

'Ah, that is better, I am getting used to having a body again, even if it is transparent,' he said, while appearing in front of William.

'Who are you?' asked William.

'Don't you recognise me or my voice? I thought you at least would remember me.'

'All I see is a ghost ...'

'Let's get it straight. I am not a ghost, I am a poltergeist and I enjoy playing games, which is why I am here.'

William looked at the poltergeist carefully and

suddenly he recognised him. 'You're Trevor van Gossenburg. We all thought you had gone back to Belgium, or was it the Netherlands, after you disappeared without saying goodbye.'

'Oh, I did not leave, my friend; unfortunately I died here in Trentby.'

'How ... what ... when ... how?' William stuttered.

'I was murdered ...'

'What do you mean, murdered?' William interrupted rudely.

'If you would stop interrupting I will tell you.'

'Alright tell me,' William said resigned to his fate.

'And don't interrupt or I will go out into the church and dirty all your brass for your cleaner.'

'I won't interrupt, I promise.'

'Good ... where shall I start? Ah yes ...'

Cavalry Cabs' office   CMH

'Welcome to Cavalry Cabs. We get you there on time,' the automated voice said before being interrupted by the controller, Pat Walker.

'Good morning, Pat Walker here. How can Cavalry Cabs help you today?' she said into the mouthpiece on her headset and then listened for a short while. 'Six cars to pick up the Mayor and bridal party at the Clement Attlee Tower block for a wedding at the Bleeding Heart on Saturday at twelve. Yes, we can do that, Lady Britney. But blue ribbons on the cars, Lady Britney? Surely you mean white, the symbol of purity? Oh, of course, Tory blue!'

Just then the power went off, the lights went out

and the computer crashed. Undaunted and struggling to find a pen and paper in the dim twilight of the office Pat continued. 'Then to take the party to the football ground for the ceremonial kick-off.'

Paper and a battered ball-point pen found and scribbling away like mad she continued, 'Other than for contract clients our terms are strictly cash you understand? But, seeing as it's a wedding, and it's for Sir Lancelot, we'll accept his cheque on the day. Thank you, Lady Britney. We'll see you on Saturday.' Unfortunately, the power interruption was only at Pat's end which meant a crucial part of the message was misheard.

Pressing the cut-off button she turned to the door and yelled, 'Hoppy, you steaming, idiotic prat! You've blown the ruddy fuses again! Get 'em fixed and get yourself down to Grants, the undertakers. That funeral's in three-quarters of an hour. Then you're wanted at the station for eleven o'clock for that medical consignment pick-up. You can prat around with that wretched cab after that! What's wrong with it now anyway?'

The answer - if there was one, because you didn't answer Pat back if she yelled at you - was interrupted by the phone ringing. Owing to the lack of space in the office - the cleaners had turned it down as too small for a store cupboard - the desk was swept clear by an errant sleeve and the paperwork, as Hopalong would say, 'Ended up on the dog shelf.'

'Good morning, Pat Walker here. How can Cavalry Cabs help you today?' she repeated into the mouthpiece on her headphones. 'Dusty! How can I help *you*?' Her voice softened as she listened to her heart throb.

'Saturday. Two cabs to the Bleeding Heart for twelve. *For you darling anything!* Pick me up this evening about eight and we'll have a drink, *or something*, and discuss a merger.' Neither of them thought that the sort of merger she was referring to would have anything to do with taxi cabs.

Hopalong, who had overheard the remark as he came in to report that it was a power cut not a blown fuse, thought otherwise.

Monday 12.30   SMS

'I say, our Vera, I say. Have you got your ears switched on?'

Vera, whose top-set was still eluding her, grinned a gap-toothed grin as the figure taking her coat off emerged into the portacabin's client-waiting-area-cum-phone-in-service office.

'Eh up, our Gloria whar're you doing here? You're a bit previous.'

'I was feeling a bit low so I thought I'd drop by and bring you a bit of something nice to do you good.' Gloria opened a shopping bag on wheels and drew out a casserole dish. 'It's still warm,' she ventured, lifting the lid as the smell of liver and onion gravy permeated the portacabin.

Vera was torn. One the one hand Bertha would go spare if she came in and found the client waiting area stinking of onion gravy but on the other hand it was half past twelve and well past her lunch time and besides they didn't have any clients waiting and she was hungry. Gloria fetched two spoons from the sink in the loo-cum-kitchenette.

'What her don't know won't hurt her, will it our kid?' grinned Gloria as both she and her cousin weighed into the hotpot with gusto.

The phone rang. It was answered by Vera with a pained expression and a mouth full of gravy. 'He-llo, Lady Vee, your Goddess of the Afternoon. How may I help you into paradise?' she spluttered.

'Oh hello, Bertha. No, no, I'm not eating anything?' she replied, her eyes watering as she swallowed a chunk of half-chewed best lamb's liver. 'Where are you? Ohhh, how lovely. I wish I was there. Are you try-ing on anything nice? I bet you are. What time are you back? That soon. Righto … No worries.'

Jabbing a spoon into the pot Vera relayed the glad tidings. 'She's on her way back. Twenty minutes. Best open the window.'

'Where from?'

'The pokey. She's put up bail for Angie and they've called in at Madam Mordebt Chappoo. You know … that new hat shop in the market square.'

'That'll be pricey,' said Gloria, mopping gravy off the bristles on her chin with the back of her cuff. 'Madam Mordebt! What a phony. Her inner French you know! Oldham born and bred!'

'Gorra have a new hat for the wedding though, hasn't her?'

'Does our Honour the Mayor know her's going?'

'Don't be daft. He can hardly stop her though, can he? She knows far too much about our "Gentleman

Jim" for comfort.'

'Besides she is the bridegroom's new step-mother's mother.'

'More to the point is who's Lady Britney's father, if you ask me,' grinned Vera adjusting the spaghetti-like string attached to her hearing aid as the phone rang again. 'He-llo, Lady Vee, your Goddess of the Afternoon. How may I help you into paradise?'

Later that Monday   SMS

'Hello, Vera, old girl ... you still at it? Haven't you got a home to go to?' said the sneer as Inspector Bruce Wallace Mackay, head of Trentby's Vice-Squad slithered through the open door of the portacabin. 'It's way past your bedtime isn't it, hen?'

'I'm waiting for a taxi. Billy's a bit tied up.'

'Billy the Kid? Good Lord above. He's a bit long in the tooth to be driving, isn't he? He must be over eighty. You make sure you strap yourself in aunty and keep you eye on the clock. No speeding, mind. And wrap up, it's dreich out tonight.'

The phone rang. Inwardly Vera groaned as the height-challenged Scotsman settled himself down on the chaise rubbing his hands. It wasn't going to be a short visit.

'He-llo there ... Lady Vee, your Goddess of the Night ... How may I help you into paradise? Oh, it's you, Vicar. Can you call back, dear? Only I've got the Vice-Squad here again at the moment? Give me ten minutes. Yes, dear, put the kettle on. Think happy thoughts. Put the baby oil in the microwave.'

Mackay spluttered into his fag packet as, patting her stone-carved perm, Vera replaced the handset and swivelled round to give him her full attention.

'Who the hell was that?'

'My lips are sealed, dearie. This is a discreet, confidential service as well you know.'

'So what "service" does the vicar want then?' pressed Mackay, lighting up and coughing as smoke trickled through the 'dead mouse' moustache which twitched alarmingly under his nose.

'Nasty cough that!' Vera said. 'Best put it away, dearie! It's against Health and Safety you know. Could get me into trouble with the police.'

Mackay grinned. 'Now would I do that? Where's Olga tonight then?' he whispered casually revealing the reason for his visit. It was common knowledge that the leggy Ukrainian was getting the better of his professional and personal judgement. Inspector Comb-over, as the girls called him, was becoming a laughing-stock in Trentby nick.

'You know I can't divulge personal information about our clients, Inspector. She's not here. She's working.'

'The Masonic do at the George Hotel, y'ken?'

Vera's eyes widened like saucers. Three of the agency's top girls were filling their faces and their handbags at the Masonic Annual Dinner. How did Old Greasy Chops know that? Weren't Masonic dos supposed to be secret? Then the penny dropped. Police ... Masons ... ahhh, yes.

The phone rang.

'He-llo, Lady Vee, your Goddess of the ... oh, hello

Bertha ... no, I'm still waiting for Billy the Kid, I'll give him a few more minutes but after the vicar's been sorted I'm off home. That nice Inspector Mackay's here on the settee again asking after Olga. Perhaps he'll drop me off, eh?'

Staring at the threadbare matting Mackay shook his head at the unbridled cheek. Aunty Vee was a character all right; they broke the mould after this old biddy popped out. But, as luck would have it, she lived on the way towards the George Hotel, didn't she? He could wait for Olga to surface and follow her and her punter. You never know, he might get lucky, she might go straight home to her flat in Clem Attlee Towers, and if she did, he could sit outside her windows and hope to catch a glimpse of her drawing the blinds. How sad was that? He had to get a grip.

Hardly had the handset rested in the cradle than the phone was ringing again.

'He-llo, Lady Vee, your Goddess of the Night. How may I help you into paradise? Oh, it's you again, Vicar. Are you sitting comfortably? Right, then we can begin.'

TUESDAY

Chummy and the reception   EH

'Father, you said I should book the reception and I have, and there was simply nowhere else.'

'But, Jason, the Labour Club! Was there nothing Independent, or even Liberal, available?'

'With the match and this being a last minute booking? No Father there wasn't.'

Lady Britney, smiling at her stepson, said, 'You've catered for 200 guests haven't you Chummy?' Jason's head started to droop. 'You have, haven't you?' she asked hopefully.

'Well,' he said brightly, 'the function room holds 170.'

'And pray,' asked his bewildered father, 'where do we put the other thirty? Or are we expecting them to stand?'

Jason hated it when his father treated him as if he were stupid. 'Of course not! I've arranged for them to be seated in the bar.'

'Oh, that makes it all right then,' said his father sarcastically.

'Yvonne said that thirty of her side could go in the bar, they won't mind at all.'

'Well, they wouldn't,' he said. 'Will the bar be at least closed to the general public?'

'No, sir.' Jason was feeling distinctly uneasy now. 'But the steward said that there won't be many in till after the match.'

'Lord Chumleigh looked at his son and once more wondered about the blood line. 'The reception, son, *is* after the match.'

'Oh,' said a deflated Jason.

Lady Britney, determined to get her husband off the seating arrangements, said, 'What about food, Chummy?'

'Oh Britney, now that is exciting. I've managed to get a French chef.'

'Now that,' said his father jumping in, 'is sounding hopeful. What do we eat then? Do tell!'

'Escargot to start, ragoût de lapin and a traditional bread and butter pudding to follow,' he said smilingly.

'So we get snails, rabbit stew and wet bread, lovely, Jason. It gets better and better.'

Throwing her husband a dirty look, Lady Britney said kindly, 'Will Yvonne's family be okay with that menu, Chummy?'

'Oh, just tell them there's plenty of brown sauce,' said her husband. 'They'll eat anything covered in that.'

'Really,' shouted Lady Britney, 'you are so snobbish sometimes!'

'There's one, slight ... erm ... problem, Father,' Jason faltered.

'Only one Jason? Well, I suppose we should be grateful for that.' Lady Britney gave her husband another withering look.

'The car park has already been booked out for a rally.'

'So when our friends turn up in their Rollers and

Bentleys they'll have to park them on the nearby council estate. Have I got that right, Jason?'

'I've sorted that out too, father. The steward's two sons, Dave and Derek, are going to patrol the streets for twenty quid each.'

Lady Britney wanted a drink. 'Chummy dear,' she said, 'that's not Dave and Derek Dodd?' She asked hopefully, remembering the terrible twosome from secondary school.

'I've done my best,' Jason shouted as he jumped up from his chair.

'It'll be all right, Chummy,' said Britney soothingly. 'You'd best go, there's still lots to be done.'

Jason, somewhat mollified, left the room feeling his father's stare on his back the whole time.

'Lord Chumleigh stood up. 'I must go, Britney, but let me tell you this. Your stepson is a moron.'

Catering for Jim   CMH

'Jim, I don't mind a quid pro quo now and again, it keeps things moving along sweetly, doesn't it? But you're asking for a fifty quid pro quo!' Bill Evans, the senior catering tutor at Trentby College of Further Education, held up his hand to stop Jim Jones from speaking. 'Yes, I can, in theory and I must stress the theory bit ask my pupils to come in on Saturday and do a lavish spread for you, but that's the day of the match. As you know; because you arranged it! All the lads have got tickets for it. It's not so much a sticky wicket, as a super-glued one!'

'Bill, I'm not having my Yvonne's wedding spoiled

for a lack of cash. We've sorted something like this before. Offer them that fifty quid each, cash in hand, I'll pay for it out of my own pocket. If you can do the spread preparation in the morning and just finish off after the match would that do it? As many free drinks as they like after the knife and fork do? Would that help? Legless for free and fifty quid on top can't be too bad, can it?'

Bill sighed. 'Well, Jim, I'll put it to them this afternoon. If I can get a dozen of the good ones it's possible. I can't say any fairer than that. I'll let you know this evening. Make sure your answer-phone's switched on! I'll sort a menu afterwards but on the face of it, it looks like escargot to start, ragoût de lapin as a main course and a traditional bread and butter pudding to follow.'

'Dunno about that ess-cargo stuff, Bill. It looks like snails to me. But I expect Chummy's lot'll eat it; they eat anything with garlic in, and the bread pudding sounds okay, as long as there's lots of custard. Proper custard mind not café custard. What's this ragoodewhatsit stuff? I hope it's a curry because I can't stand that sweet and sour stuff. Gives me the wind something chronic does sweet and sour. Anyway, why a funny menu like that, Bill?'

Bill gave a short sharp bark of what was almost laughter. 'That's easy. Given the dopey lot we've got this year that's about all they're capable of doing. Anything other than simple stuff's beyond them and we've got most of the ingredients in the fridges. I think Bert, sorry Luigi, must have ordered them for some reason.'

Jim looked at his watch. 'Heavens is that the time? Sorry I can't stop here chatting Bill, got a committee meeting to get to five minutes ago.' So saying he exited the tiny office in a hurry, leaving a bemused Bill shaking his head in sorrow.

Half way down the corridor he pulled a brick-sized mobile phone out of his pocket and contacted his wife. 'Got the feast sorted, Jan,' he told her, 'Ess-cargo to start with. Like that stuff we had when that French delegation came over last year, then some foreign stuff called ragoo-day-lap-Anne or somethin' and bread and butter pudding as a sweet. Goin' to cost us a bit though. Sorted it is. So much for that wally Lancelot. Couldn't organise a ... ermm ... you know what I mean. Couldn't find his backside with two hands and a map.'

Janice wasn't so sure. She told herself she must meet up with Lady Britney and make sure these men aren't making fools of themselves, again!

All the news   SMS

Philip Bonnay scratched behind his ear with a pencil and typed on his keyboard with one hand faster than most folks can with two.

'Any joy with the lovely illegal immigrant?' asked a familiar voice in the editorial office of the *Trentby Evening News*. 'She still a contender for Page Three? Hey, that's a headline for you: 'Illegal Immigrants in Illegal Vice-racket ... Illegal Strip Off!'

'Early days yet, Chris. But promising.'

'Full of eastern promise ... if you ask me,' replied

the chief reporter, Christopher Cross.

'I didn't,' murmured Bonnay under his breath. There was no love lost between the two rivals. Cross had once been on the Canary Wharf nationals and had fallen on hard times. He considered Trentby to be a retrograde step in the train wreck that was his career, whereas Bonnay had been up-and-coming until Cross had snaffled the 'chief' job out from under his nose. Exposing the discreet personal services being offered by Bertha's harem of exotic beauties would be a scoop which would shake the Trentby establishment. It would do his career no harm at all.

'If it's too much for you, kiddo, you can call on me to take over at any time,' smirked Cross, slithering away towards the coffee machine.

Pausing only for a quick spray with the breath freshener, Bonnay reached for the phone.

It was answered by the liquid vowels of Lady Vee. He heard her call him a Frenchie as she passed the phone to Olga. Strange to relate but when Olga Romanovski said, ''ello, Philip,' in that incredibly desirable accent, his knees turned to water and his collar started to strangle him, and, later when she agreed to meet him in half an hour on the canal side by the lock gates, he snuck out of the *Evening News'* dog-eared apology for an editorial office walking on balloons.

Goings-on at The Mansions MH

William poured himself another Jack Daniels and sat looking at Trevor.

'Do you know it drives me mad when I see people eating and drinking, I really miss the taste,' moaned Trevor.

'It must be annoying,' William agreed.

'I tried some of your whisky earlier, it dripped through my jaw onto the floor. It was worse when I tried to eat some strawberries, they rattled around my ribcage like a pinball machine. You should have seen the look on the greengrocer's face when he saw them dropping on the floor,' he laughed.

'You are supposed to be ethereal, aren't you. So tell me how could strawberries rattle around inside you?' William asked.

'No idea. They just did.'

'Anyway, you were going to explain what happened to you!'

'Yes, sorry, I digress. When I came to England I went to work for Sir Lancelot to train his racehorses. I had a lot of success back home so when the job offer came, I decided to come over here and try my luck. At first everything was perfect and a filly called Britney Tears I was training began showing a lot of promise and was expected to do well. Unfortunately, that is when Lady Britney began to take an interest in the horses, particularly the filly named after her.

'What happened?' William asked.

'To begin with she was very formal and seemed genuinely interested in my training methods, but as the weeks passed she spent more and more time in the stables and she began to flirt with me.'

'Oh no, Trevor, don't tell me you flirted as well?' William asked.

'What could I do, I had recently finished with my girlfriend after she had run off with that footballer. She left me because he had a big ... '

'I don't want to hear ...', William interrupted quickly.

'I was going to say "big bank balance", what did you think I was going to say?' Trevor asked.

'Sorry, I thought you were about to tell me about a part of his anatomy,' William admitted.

'Yeah, like I know.'

'Come on, carry on with your story,' William cajoled.

'She began wearing sexy outfits and revealing plenty of flesh every time she came to see me until I couldn't resist any longer and I had to dip my wick.'

'Dip your wick?'

'Willie, I am not going to spell it out for you.'

'Oh ... that, okay, c-c-carry on,' he stuttered as he thought of his fairy outfit.

'Our affair quickly moved to her bedroom and every time Sir Lancelot left on business we would spend time there. We had great fun and I began to fall for her in a big way - and told her so. She told me she was also in love with me and we planned to run away together.'

'Then how did you die if you were leaving with her?' William asked with a frown.

'Now, there's a story I would prefer not to tell!'

Angela's assets   SMS

'Ethel, is that you? Goodness, gal, that health spa makeover has worked wonders. You look terrific,' replied Vera, rapidly changing the subject away from Olga's new boyfriend.

'Sasha! How many more times, Vera! It's Sasha! I don't want my clients hearing me called Ethel, do I?' spluttered the Amazonian six-footer whose new chin-job had been sewn up so high it was pulling down her eyebrows and whose stilettos could have been classed as dangerous weapons in other circumstances. 'Sounds like a Saxon princess! Now, there's a thought! What do you think, Angie? Plaits and a sword? Shield-maiden?'

Ethel was followed into the portacabin's client waiting area by the generous matronly figure of Angela Cuthbuttwright, housemother to the inmates of Number 27, who was having a little difficulty containing the contents of her blouse and had both hands presently engaged adjusting the under wiring.

'Forty-eight quid and it's a piece of junk. Ruddy measured for this flipping contraption, I was. Falling out all over the place.'

'Yes, dear, but *when* was you measured for it?' asked Gloria helpfully sniffing at the overpowering display of fluffy pink pillows Angela was optimistically attempting to squeeze back inside the corsetry, which was clearly several sizes too small.

'You can't get the genie back in that bottle, pet.' agreed Vera sagely. 'Give up and put the kettle on.'

Hardly were the words out of her mouth than the phone rang.

'He-llo, Lady Vee, your Goddess of the Afternoon. How may I help you into paradise? Hey up! Hello, Headmaster. Long time no ... calm down, dear. Calm down. You've done what? Now that was a silly boy, wasn't it? It's *one* little blue tablet. Not *six*. Yes it will, dear – think limp thoughts. It'll be like that for some time, dear. Don't shout at me. It's not my fault you've taken too many. Cover it up with something. I don't know what, do I? A teacloth if you like, cover it up with a teacloth. Keep it hidden under your desk. Call me later if you like when it's a bit more manageable. We got a special offer on at the moment: BOGOF.' Vera held the handset away from her ear as a wave of shouted expletives boiled over from the earpiece and filled the room. Vera cradled it with a wide-eyed expression.

'Is that what they mean by a sound bite? Not a happy camper?' said Ethel, smoothing a sunset-yellow miniskirt under her ample posterior as she perched on the chaise and searched for a ciggie in the cavernous depths of a leopard-skin handbag only the size of Hampshire.

'Silly old soul, another Blackpool Tower ... over done the little blue pills ... fancied a quick one and forgot all about the governors' meeting,' explained Vera, clearly pained that one of her old boys was in trouble.

'Easy mistake to make,' tittered Angie as with a flourish out whooshed the offending scaffolding of the 'bosom holster' from beneath the frilly blouse allowing impressive assets free to wobble unencumbered. The joyous bid for freedom was such a seismic event that the cabin walls trembled in shock. 'Eee, that's better.'

'It certainly is from where I'm standing,' said a

voice from the doorway and Doc Hollyweigh wandered in grinning. 'Right, who ordered a cab? Hello, is that kettle on? I've just got time for a quick one. It might be my last, them beggars at the Council want us all to take eye tests.'

One of our cabs is missing   JP

Reluctantly, Tony Wyatt took another bite of his sandwich. 'BLT', he muttered to himself. 'Whoever thought of putting cold bacon with lettuce and tomato sure wasn't born in Staffordshire. Anyone born in Staffordshire knows bacon should be eaten sizzling with eggs, cheese and oatcakes. BLT – Bloody Lousy Taste, more like.

But it wasn't just the quality of his lunch that depressed Tony. It was, well, everything. Here he was, 23-years-old with a degree in media studies and catering and the only job he could get after two years out of Trentby University was driving for Cavalry Cabs. Living with his mum was driving him mad, he had a student debt of twenty grand and the last time he had an intimate relationship with a woman was after he'd watched Trentby United from the old wooden stand and a young nurse at A&E had to remove a splinter from his left buttock.

'Ah, well. Suppose I'd better get back to it,' he sighed, throwing the remains of his sandwich to the three ducks circling the edge of the park lake in anticipation. He walked down the path to the gate in Park Avenue where he'd parked his cab, slowing just enough to take in an uplifting glimpse of the girls from Trentby College of Further Education playing tennis. As he passed through the gate, he casually took his car key from his pocket and pressed the remote locking button. His thoughts on why whoever designed the sports skirt hadn't been given at least one Nobel Prize were interrupted when he realized his cab hadn't answered.

He pressed the remote again. The little light flashed but there were no comforting bleeps in response. He looked up. He'd definitely parked his cab behind that pink convertible with the 'If you don't like my driving, stay off the pavement' sticker but it wasn't there now. Then, with the sharp mind of a man with a degree in media studies and catering, Tony realized: 'I've lost the bloody cab!'

'Lost the cab? Lost the cab? How the blazes can you lose a cab?' Pat Walker hollered down the phone. 'It's not a pesky paper clip. Anybody can lose a paper clip. This is a big blue thing with wheels and a picture of John Wayne in *Fort Apache* on the side.'

'Sorry, Pat,' stuttered Wyatt. 'When I say I've lost it, I mean somebody's nicked it.'

'Oh, somebody's nicked it, have they? That makes me feel so much better. No wonder the lads call you Wyatt Twerp. You're a prize twerp. I don't suppose you know who this somebody might be?'

'No, not really. There was nobody about in Park Avenue when I parked up. Just one of them Concorde Cabs pulling away a bit further down the road.'

'A Concorde Cab? Did you see who was driving it?'

'Sorry, Pat, It was too far away. D'you think they've got something to do with it?'

'I wouldn't put it past 'em. One of 'em nicked Ho-palong's crematorium job on Monday. I'll have a quiet word with Dusty at Concorde Cabs. See if he knows anything. You stay where you are and I'll get one of the lads to pick you up. Twerp!'

Pat was pretty sure she knew Dusty Miller well enough to know when he was lying to her so when he said Wyatt's missing cab had nothing to do with Concorde drivers, then it hadn't. Or it had, thought Pat, but Dusty hadn't heard about it yet. But, with the insurance claim in mind, there was nothing else she could do now except ring the police.

Later that evening

'Trentby Police are looking for a taxi cab that went missing earlier today from outside the town's Victoria Park. A police spokesperson said they have not ruled out the possibility of a turf war among local taxi firms. The cab is a dark blue Toyota Avensis, registration ...'

Dave Dodd switched off the *Midlands News* and reached for his mobile phone. 'Eh, Derek, get over here. Christmas and yer birthday have come at once.'

Painful memories   MH

'Come on, Trevor, tell me about how you died,' ordered William.

'Do I have too? It brings back painful memories in more ways than one,' said Trevor sadly.

'It is up to you, I suppose. However, I would have thought it would be better to get it off your chest ... if you had one,' said William, trying to be funny.

'That was not funny; you aren't the one who died.'

'Look, Trev, if you are not going to tell me, I have work to do. Sir Lancelot's son is getting married on Saturday.'

'Oh, I know, going to be the marriage of the year. I don't think so,' Trevor said in a strangely evil voice.

'What do you mean by that comment?' William asked cagily.

'Nothing. Forget I said anything. Shall I tell you how I died?' Trevor replied a little too quickly, which didn't go unnoticed by William.

'Go on, let's hear it.'

'It all happened on a Wednesday afternoon six months ago; Sir Lancelot had gone into town, something to do with the election. So within a couple of minutes of him leaving, Lady Britney and I were in the sack.'

'Sack?' interrupted the vicar.

'For heaven's sake, Willie, it means "in bed".'

'Oh, I thought perhaps it was some sort of sexual deviation.'

'Yeah, right, a comment like that coming from a man who wears fairy outfits. Will you please let me continue?'

'Yes, sorry, go ahead.'

'We were "in bed" when I heard a slight noise on the stairs, I immediately panicked and jumped out of bed, pulled my trousers on as I ran out of the room. Lady Britney looked at me, smiled and shouted, 'Good luck, you're gonna need it.'

'That was a strange thing to say,' William commented.

'Come to think of it, it was. Anyway on the stairs stood Sir Lancelot with a devilish grin aimed in my direction. Without giving him chance to say anything I ran down the stairs two at a time before making my escape out of the French windows, which were open - luckily. I ran across the courtyard and jumped over the fence into one of the fields and headed towards the nearby copse. I ran as fast as I could but for a man his age Lancelot was remarkably quick. I had age and fitness on my side until suddenly, as I was looking back over my shoulder to see if he was catching up, I tripped over a low wall and felt myself floating through the air. Weightless and flying like a bird in the sky. I stretched out my arms and soared. It was wonderful.'

'Then what happened?'

'I landed in icy water. I'd accidentally thrown myself off the edge of the Trentby mainline viaduct where it crosses the River Trent.'

'Ouch, that must have been a painful experience,' laughed William. 'It's over a hundred feet high over by Lord Chumleigh's place.'

'Very funny, Willie, I don't think.' Trevor shouted angrily. 'You cannot imagine how that unfortunate event changed my life. I was toast. Gone! I was no more. Cream crackered. Washed out to sea.'

'I should be more caring. I apologise,' said William through clenched teeth while trying not to laugh.

Rays of sunshine   SMS

'Morning, Aunty Vera. Zat kettle still iz warm, iz it not?'

'Hey up, our Olga, you're up, and about early, aren't you, pet? It's only ten o'clock. You got an early riser booked?'

Olga pulled a leather Goth coat firmly round her sylph-like frame and waved a chipped mug in Vera's direction. She was clearly not herself. When she removed the purple sunglasses it looked to Vera's professionally trained eye as if the Ukrainian girl had been crying.

'You not well, dearie? What's the matter? You can tell me.'

Olga sank on to the battered chaise her thigh-high, stiletto-heeled boots creasing about the back of the knees and the lines of hearts on her purple tights disappearing like miners going underground under the hem of a pillar-box red miniskirt which was stretching its seams beyond endurance.

'E was zere again last night,' she said by way of reply. ''e iz always zere. 'E iz stalking me. And who can I turn to when it is a policeman who iz doing ziz?'

'There's no harm in him, dearie. He's just a bit nuts about you. He wouldn't hurt a hair on that pretty head of yours, I'm sure.'

The phone rang just as the kettle was coming to the boil. 'He-llo, Lady Vee, your Goddess of the Morning. How may I help you into paradise? Oh hello, Your Honour. The special offer is it? BOGOF. Have you got a new credit card, Judge? Oh good. Give me the big number and then we'll see what we can do.'

As Vera's silken patter worked its magic, Olga paced by the window nursing the coffee mug and staring out over the wasteland that was Trentby Enterprise industrial estate, on a wet Tuesday morning. Sure enough parked over by the recycling centre was the black beamer and behind the wheel was the pulled-down baseball cap of Inspector Bruce Wallace Mackay.

'There you are, dearie that's better isn't it? Call back later for the freebie. It's in the book, don't worry. You'll get your money's worth,' finished Vera twisting a corkscrew curl round her finger as she cradled the handset. 'That's my good deed for the day. Put His Lordship in a good mood for Crown Court.' Olga grinned, Vera could cheer anybody up.

'Forget the 'Comb-over King,' tell me about last night.'

'Zer was the "ruck-tions" iz that ze word? Yes? Ruck-tions! The big wedding iz in big trouble. Ze chief executive of ze council, he dropped me off and went 'ome ... he'z never done that before.'

'What? Why? What's happened?' cried Vera, her hands springing to her cheeks in horror.

'Zey were all talking about ze crash ... and the reception being off ... no cake ... no flowerz ... no 'otel booking ... no band ... no limozeen ... It vas so upzetting. The Mayor and Zir Lancelot they were shouting at each other and zere ladies were crying.'

'What, Lady Britney? In tears? Oh, my mother's laundry ... does Bertha know? There'll be hell up.'

The phone rang breaking into Vera's foreboding. 'He-llo, Lady Vee, your Goddess ... yes, Bertha, I've just heard the caterers have gone bust ... You what? They've done what? The rotters ... done a runner with the deposit. They must have known for weeks ... What's to do? Oh, yes, right ...You carry on. I'll hold the fort.'

Olga rubbed the steamy window pane. The beamer was moving off. She was free of her tail for a while. Just as well because she had a date. An unofficial, unpaid date, which if Bertha knew about she would not be happy.

The phone rang as Vera was trying to take a sip of her third cuppa that morning.

'He-llo, Lady Vee, your Goddess of the Morning. How may I ... Who ... Philip who? Olga, it's for you. Philip Bonnay, whoever he is when he's at home? Sounds like some Frenchie.'

Olga just smiled as she reached for the handset and suddenly the sun peaked from behind a cloud and it stopped raining.

The American connection   CMH

Over the breakfast table, Sir Lancelot looked at the morning post and snarled, 'Who the Dickens invited Wychita Wainwright-Wilberforce III to your wedding Jason? I know he's a cousin of yours, twice removed on your mother's side or something, and he's got an enormous pile of cash, but this is too flaming much. W3's a world-class prat!'

'Oh, I don't know. The last time he was here I thought he was rather sweet,' chipped in Britney. 'That ex-wife of his is tarted up mutton-dressed-as-lamb that I wouldn't trust out of sight; but he's okay.'

'Well, you did say that I needed all the help I could get,' said Jason. 'Big W3 is okay. He's letting us have his backwoods shack for our honeymoon and he's insisted on paying for our airfare. At least that's what I think he meant. Said that "arranging our transportation" was his wedding present.'

Lancelot snorted and snarled. 'I've seen his "backwoods shack!" His little ranch he calls it; there's more marble there than at Versailles. It's in 320 square miles of land, ten miles off the main road with a dozen live-in staff and its own power station. From one side of the pool to the other is a three day horse ride, you need a satellite phone to order breakfast and his blasted idea of a light snack is a flaming five-course meal! The man's an idiot and a menace to organised society but that's beside the point. The point is, who asked the idiot along?'

'I'm not sure,' Jason replied. 'I mean ... I know I was emailing him about things you asked me to research ... and I did mention that I was getting married. You know the things you say off the cuff.'

Britney chipped in, 'You know, Lance, things like saying, "You must drop in sometime" when you know that people won't. Well, not Trenby people anyway, they know you're only being polite.'

Lancelot glared at both of them. 'So he's invited himself, then ... and I suppose we'll have to put him up? You know what Avis thinks about our "Cute little town house" and the lack of a helipad in the grounds. What about your car, Britney? You remember what she said about that? "Gee, honey, what a cute little car you have, I don't know why you don't get a real one" or something, wasn't it? You were using the station wagon at the time.'

Taking a deep breath to calm himself he continued, 'They can have the blue bedroom again. We know the bed will stand the weight, and her maid can have one of the old staff rooms. Arrange to get somebody in to clean them up will you, dear?'

'At the least, Father, it'll help with your re-election campaign. You know; the foreign affairs bit. You can tell the papers you're "Working with world trade leaders to foster understanding" and all that guff. No need to tell anybody who he really is. Is there?'

'When and where are they arriving, Lance?' Britney asked. 'They'll need meeting at the airport and help with their luggage surely?'

After another perusal of the offending letter, Lancelot shook his head. 'The cretin doesn't say. Just that he'll be here on Thursday or Friday, probably in the morning, on his way back from an Indian and African business tour.' He busied himself with a knife and fork. 'He doesn't mention the ex-wife in here — perhaps he's finally ditched the leech.'

'Chummy!' Britney commanded, 'Get on the phone and get the details. You know the kind of thing, which airport, when, flight number, etcetera. I'll get some food and temporary staff organised.' She stood up, and, tightly denim-clad hips swaying provocatively, walked out.

Councillor Peacock   SMS

'Hey up, our Vera, you'll never guess what I've just seen on the towpath!' spluttered Gloria wiggling her shopping basket in through the door of the porta-cabin and wafting a drenched umbrella about with gusto.

'Mind out, Gloria, you'll get them Special Offer fly-ers soggy,' reprimanded Vera, who was on a comfort break and had the kettle in hand. 'So what have you been up to, then?'

'Not me. That Olga. She's up to no good. Mark my words.'

'Olga? She's only just left. She's on a day off. I think.'

'Freelancing if you ask me,' said Gloria, slumping down on the chaise and taking off soggy sandals. Rubbing her bunions with heartfelt relief, she added, 'Very odd, I could have sworn I knew that bloke from some-where. It'll come back to me. Gloria Allerdyce never forgets a face.'

Hardly had Vera sat down than the phone rang.

'He-llo, Lady Vee, your Goddess of the Afternoon. How may I help you into paradise? Oh, hello, Councillor Peacock, back again. You're getting your full quota of the Special Offer aren't you dearie? And why not? Wife at her sister's again, is she?'

Gloria's eyes rolled towards the ceiling. Ernie Pea-cock would surely still be at work at the funeral par-lour at this time of day. Seemed a little incongruous be-haviour for anyone in a mourning rig but who was she to comment? Vera was signed up on Bertha's bonus-related time and motion productivity deal after all. The more clients she catered for in an hour, the more percentages dropped into their holiday fund. Holiday fund. That was it. That was him. That was who she had seen stalking Olga and that pink-faced lad from the *Evening News*. It was that reporter from the *News of the Times*. The one from Pootlins. She could hardly contain her excitement until Vera had finished sorting out the undertaker's dubious desires. It wouldn't be long now, her cousin was panting so fast she'd need oxygen if she wasn't careful, but then she had got an inhaler handy just in case.

'Thank heavens for that. Seven minutes flat! You'll be in *The Guinness Book of Records* at this rate,' grinned Gloria, as red-faced Vera cradled the handset and took a swig of tea.

'I had to get a move on, he'd got a service booked at half past.'

'Never mind Ernie Peacock, it was him. That reporter from Pootlins.'

'Who?'

'The bloke following Olga and that young man of hers.'

'And what young man would that be?' said a familiar voice entering the portacabin. Fortunately, it was only Ethel, so no harm was done.

Dusty takes time out to reflect   JP

In Concorde Cab's office, Dusty was having a moment to himself, and while dunking a soggy, chocolate di-

gestive into a mug of PG, allowing thoughts of a con-
jugal nature to wander back to the previous Saturday
evening ...

Pat Walker struggled to open her eyes. 'Dusty?'
she murmured. The closing music of *Match of the
Day* was bellowing out of the rented TV in the corner
of her living room as she raised her voice, 'Dusty.' It
only seemed five minutes ago that Starsky was
bombing around the city streets of California with
Hutch in their red Ford Gran Torino and now here
was the curly hunk scoring the winning goal for Liverpool.

Well, maybe it wasn't him; but nice legs she
thought as she tried to get the blood flowing in her
right arm.

It was the same every Saturday evening. She and
Dusty always arranged to finish work at six on a Saturday.
They'd meet in the High Street for a meal. It was either
The Crown for prawn cocktail, chicken-in-the-basket
with Black Forest gateau and a couple of pints of
Trentby Torpedo Bitter, or the First Emperor Chinese
restaurant for the three-course banquet with coffee
at £7.50 a head, washed down with a bottle of Blue
Nun. Then back to Pat's for the *Val Doonican Show*
and the inevitable end to a day that had seen them
both up at five o'clock to get on the taxi switchboards
by six.

'Dusty!' yelled Pat, fully awake now and impatiently
scanning the sofa around her. Slowly there was
movement and Dusty Miller's head emerged from
Pat's cavernous cleavage with the expression of a
man who had won Littlewood's Treble Chance, been

picked to play for England and discovered he had inherited Paul Getty's millions all on the same day.

'That's the trouble with you, Dusty. You never listen to a word I say,' grumbled Pat.

'Strange that,' said the diminutive Dusty, looking at Pat's magnificent bosom like a dormouse who's just found a nesting place for the winter, 'every time I get my head down there I seem to go deaf.'

Pat had always been a big girl. As a teenager she could have modelled for McGill's postcards and helped the war effort by donating her silk knickers to the RAF so they could make parachutes out of them.

That's where she first met Dusty when he was stationed just outside Trentby. They went out a couple of times but he was transferred and they lost touch. After the War, Pat married Cyril McHawtree, who by night was Gene Hawtree, Trentby's Own Singing Cowboy, never without his faithful horse Sporran, and who by day worked at the Trentby Abattoir. Cyril claimed both jobs fulfilled his boyhood ambition to work with animals. When the public's fascination moved on from singing cowboys to bingo, Cyril set up Cavalry Cabs only to meet a sad end a few months later in what was always referred to as an 'abattoir-related' accident.

Pat took over the running of the business, keeping the western theme going in Cyril's memory, and when the rival cab firm was sold a year or so later, who should take it on but her long lost Dusty. Now retired from the Air Force, Dusty renamed the business Concorde Cabs and signed up some of his ex-RAF pals as drivers.

Pat heaved herself up on the sofa. 'Ooo, you are cheeky ...' she smiled, doing her best Dick Emery voice as she slapped Dusty's shoulder, sending him sprawling on to the turquoise shag pile, '... but I like you.'

'So you should,' said Dusty, pulling himself up to his full five-foot-four, 'what with me coming back to Trentby after all those years just to find you.'

'And swept me off my feet, you did.'

'Well, hardly, replied Dusty, 'I'd have needed a couple of jeeps and a combined harvester to sweep you off you feet.' He was only halfway out of the door when something hit his shoulder and sent him stumbling into the hall.

'But *I* only need a cushion,' laughed Pat.

At that moment Dusty's reverie was destroyed by two things happening simultaneously, his digestive disintegrating into mush and the phone ringing.

'Concorde Cabs,' mumbled Dusty licking milky chocolate off his fingers. Gooey chocolate always reminded him of Pat. He'd have to get round to doing something!

The hunt for the chocolate fountain   SMS

'Now there's someone with a lot to live up to,' said Vera, casting a glance out of the window of the portacabin at the occupant of the taxi that was obviously heading their way. As she spoke the bling-clad figure of Lady Britney emerged from the rear of Hopalong's ancient black cab. Doing the dutiful driver bit to per-

fection, Hopalong, who used to be a cowboy singer in
workingmen's clubs in his younger days, and still
insisted in wearing a Stetson and cowboy boots,
scurried after her ladyship carrying a suitcase and
several shiny carrier bags with the name 'Madam
Mordebt' emblazoned on them.

'It's our Britney,' beamed Bertha who had just
spent a miserable three hours in the hairdresser's
and was recovering on the chaise with an Irish coffee
and an Eccles cake.

'Put those down over there, Hopalong, and here's
a fiver; don't put this trip on His Lordship's account,'
the madam said, patting his bottom as he tottered
on Cuban heels down the steps. 'Wait a few minutes,
there's a love, she won't be long.'

Lady Britney flopped onto the chaise, smelled the
coffee and took a sip. 'Ohh, I needed that, Mother.'

'What's in the bags, poppet?'

'It's all that stuff Chummy borrowed when he went
on his stag trip.'

'Well, that's a surprise. The moron's done something right for a change!' interrupted Vera, only to
receive a black look from Bertha who regarded the
moments she shared with her daughter from high
places as precious and private. Fortunately Vera was
saved from Bertha's scathing wit by the telephone
ringing.

'He-llo, Lady Vee, your Goddess of the Afternoon.
How may I help you into paradise? Hello Major, what
a nice surprise. I haven't had a good gallop for ages. Up
for a few jumps over Beechers are we? You've found
the plunger for your little pump then have you? Oh,

good. Where was it, dear? Under the sink with the French polish. Right, dear. Hang on a minute, I'll find the "William Tell Overture" and get the whip out. No ... not the William Tell? Oh right ... yes, of course, dear. Of course I don't mind, you're the one paying. You know our motto ... the client is always upper most in our thoughts ... if you want the theme to *Rawhide* ... you shall have the theme to *Rawhide* ... only remember what happened last time, dear. Do close the blinds in the living room. That pool cleaner could have sued and, Bertha can take no responsibility for injuries to third parties.

As strains of "Keep them dowgies movin'" drifted out of the window across to where Hopalong was snoozing, his dust-lined countenance broke out into a broad grin. 'Head 'em up, ride 'em in, Vera,' he sighed contentedly.

Meanwhile in the client waiting area and, figuratively, not wishing to put Vera off her stroke, 'How's the wedding plans going?' whispered Bertha, patting her daughter's knee. Britney stopped topping up the purloined coffee with Irish whiskey and took a deep breath.

'It'll be a disaster, Mother. I've been everywhere I can think of to hire a chocolate fountain at short notice. How can you have a wedding reception without a chocolate fountain?' A flicker of pain was etched behind those enormous false eyelashes which blinked in unison as an angelic pointy chin trembled with emotion.

'You leave that to me, poppet. Vera can make a few calls. How big do you want? Milk, or plain, or white, or perhaps a waterfall effect of all three? Very tasteful. Very tasteful with strawberries,' added Bertha, shaking her head emphatically as both her maternal instinct and her Buckingham Palace earrings went into overdrive.

Later that day

'Raw berries and gherkins? You are sure about this Vera?' asked Gloria, putting on a plastic headscarf. 'You're sure Bertha said white chocolate with raw berries and gherkins.'

'True as I'm standing here,' replied Vera fiddling with her hearing-aid. 'Perhaps it's one of those high society fads and fancies.'

'On your head, Vera, on your head! I'll nip round to our Gwendolyn and check she's still got hers. She never had chance to use it, you see. Brand new, I'll bet you, it's still all wrapped up in the boxes. Poor soul.'

'Gwen, the cleaner at the Church of the Bleeding Heart? That Gwen? The one with the … ' Vera didn't get chance to finish the sentence.

'Very clean is our Gwen. You could eat your dinner off her loo seat. Look, it'll be perfect. All we've got to do is borrow the fountain kit and buy a box of kids' chocolate and a big jar of gherkins from the cash and carry and we're laughing,' said Gloria, brooking no argument.

'Will Gwen part with it, though? It'll get dirty won't it? All that chocolate and gherkin juice? You know how she is, bless her. Especially as it was all because of the trauma of her own wedding day that it all kicked off like … ' questioned Vera sagely patting her blue-rinse back into place.

'Left at the altar, poor soul. And her with her very own chocolate fountain,' agreed Gloria applying a waft of Moonlight in Margate to her underarms with a deft whip up of her cardi.

Vera was coming over philosophical as the memories flooded back, 'It was left at the hen night actually. How was I to know her fiancé was going to be getting off with the stripper in the White Lion disco when we hens all piled in singing "OO AHH CAN-TON-AR?"'

'Stag nights have a lot to answer for!' added Gloria sagely. 'I wonder what she means by raw berries? I'll get a mixed selection from Mr Perkins, the greengrocer on the corner of Bridge Street. He's very good like that, he'll know.'

As Gloria departed the name Perkins reverberated in Vera's ears as she fiddled with the string to her hearing aid; Perkins sounded familiar. It never dawned on Vera that Bertha had actually said, "Order strawberries from Perkins" rather than "raw berries and gherkins". But then, it was a mistake anyone could have made.

At that moment the telephone rang, putting all thoughts of gherkins and chocolate fountains out of mind.

WEDNESDAY

Not the Health Service   CMH

In their respective offices Pat Walker and Dusty looked at identical letters from the local Health Authority. The important parts ran: *'As the Authority is required to show Value for Money on its services, it has been decided to terminate the current long-term, non-emergency personnel transport contracts and replace them with individual short-term contracts. Pursuant to this, your firm ... will receive a fax or phone call for an immediate journey between speci-fied addresses. A contract reference will be issued for each journey ... each reference is to be quoted on the monthly invoice. The omission of the reference will result in the disallowance of the total invoice ... separate invoices will be required for each hospital site.'*

'What's up, Dusty?' came from Ace, one of the Concorde drivers. 'Looks as if you've lost a tenner and found a sour apple.'

'You could be right, Ace. The hospitals, both of them, have dumped the contract pick-ups. From now on it's a lot of single-journey jobs with the paperwork to go in at the end of the month. We all know what that means!'

Ace pursed his lips as he thought about it. 'Well, it means somebody will have to do a lot of typing and accounts work, that's what it means! Momma's okay on that score, Biggles will be a problem and Ginger's a dead loss when it comes to paperwork. Your idea of having us being self-employed has backfired on you, old son.'

'Not really, Ace. If I got a computer and we kept up to date on it then it should be — a doddle.'

'You mean it should be unless somebody mucks it up! And anyway there's only the two of us with any sort of idea how to use one. The others are going to have to learn, and fast!'

'First thing first, Ace. I'm going up to the Health people and talk to them. They don't seem to know that Concorde is just an office set-up that hasn't got any employees. I'll have to see what I can do.'

Over at the office of Cavalry Cabs, Pat Walker was in conference with Doc Hollyweigh who was also the company secretary.

'What do you think, Doc? Do you see any problems?'

'That all depends, Pat. There shouldn't be any problem, provided the computer doesn't break down and the stuff is put in immediately. You'll need to have words with somebody about the format and, let's face it Pat, that machinery is antique. We will definitely need to be looking at a new one with up-to-date software and a better printer. One you don't have to thump to get started.'

'More expense we don't need, Doc. It's just too much hassle.' She paused in thought. 'I think I'll take up his proposal and marry Dusty. Then I'll retire to domestic bliss!'

'You? Retire? No way, my dear girl. You enjoy all of it too much to do that.'

'Maybe, Doc, maybe. But in the meantime you've got a funeral at Grants, the undertakers in twenty-five minutes, driving and pall bearing, so get changed and get across there.' Doc left with a worried look on his face.

It only hurts when I laugh   MH

'So tell me, Trevor, what happened next?' asked William excitedly.

'You're enjoying this, aren't you?' Trevor accused.

'No, not at all, I just want to know what Sir Lancelot did, and get the complete story,' he lied.

'Well, last thing I remember he was chasing me towards the copse, which I can tell you was agony, what with my asthma.'

'That must have been terrible for you,' said William, while trying to hide a snigger.

'Yes, it was, but what happened next was a shocker. I expected him to catch up to me, to have me banished from England, thrown out of the golf club, however, the rest is a blank.

'Yes, go on,' William pushed.

'Can you guess what happened next?'

'No idea at all,' William admitted.

'Aww come on, Willie. You must be able to guess,'

'Sorry, Trevor, I don't know,'

'Then you are not very observant, are you?'

'I don't understand what you mean,' William said while shaking his head.

'That dastardly baronet finished me ...' Trevor cried out. 'Or as good as. Clear off the cliff, I was driven clear off the cliff.'

'How? Did you bleed to death?' he guessed.

'Willie, you must lead a very sheltered life. People don't expire from being chased.'

'Then tell me!'

'Is there anything strange about me, something you may have missed for instance?' Trevor asked impatiently.

'Let me take a closer look at you.'

'Might be a good idea,' Trevor said sarcastically.

'OH MY, I DON'T BELIEVE IT! How could I have missed it?' William screeched.

'I can't believe you never noticed it before, after all I do have crustaceans sticking out of my head,' Trevor pointed to the crust of barnacles and limpets, garnished with seaweed that were embedded in his skull.'

'I am so sorry.' William looked stunned.

'And do you know the reason why I was accidentally drowned?'

'Of course I do.'

'It had nothing to do with me having an affair with Lady Britney; in fact he practically thanked me for helping him out in the nookie department. Apparently our Britney is a bit of a nymphomaniac and he has a great deal of trouble keeping up with her, if you know what I mean.'

'Is she really?' asked William quietly.

'Thinking of going to offer your services, Vicar? I am sure she could make up some very interesting games with your fairy outfit,' he laughed.

'I am a happily married man I will have you know,'

said William indignantly.

'Yeah, right. Anyway do you want to know why I ended up at the bottom of the viaduct?'

'Yes, tell me.'

'It was for money.'

'I don't understand, how could it be for money? You didn't have a lot I would imagine?' William commented.

'Oh, I was paid pretty well, but that isn't the reason for my untimely demise ...'

Just as Trevor was going to tell William there was a knock on his door and in walked Lady Britney.

'Hello, Vicar, thought I would come and look around your quaint little church before the nuptials.'

'You are very welcome, Your Ladyship,' he told her, while out of the corner of his eye he saw with horror the poltergeist was carrying the bottle of Jack Daniels towards Lady Britney.

Wednesday bloody Wednesday   CMH

'What do you mean, Billy? You can't find your cab? It was in the garage last night when we locked up!' The voice of Pat Walker boomed out of the office.

'Well, it's not there now!' said Billy the Kid as he came out of the workshop area. 'The place's empty except for the spare cab and that's still waiting to be fixed. Somebody's having me on and I don't like it, Pat. I ... do ... not ... like ... it ... at ... all!'

The VIP phone rang to be answered by Pat. 'Hello, this is ...' she got as far as saying when she was interrupted.

'Trentby Police here, Ms Walker,' the voice of Alan, her traffic warden next-door neighbour, who said: 'Look, Pat, I've had a report of one of your cabs, apparently abandoned, out on the Great North Road Island. Apart from somebody having been sick in the back it seems to be in perfect working order, keys in and everything. Just that there's no fuel in it. Get it shifted, will you? Before we have to tow it away and impound it.'

'Thanks, Alan. I'll get Billy to shift it straight away.' She turned and told Billy to get some fuel to it. He was simultaneously alarmed and delighted.

Over a post-work planning-meeting drink with Doc and Billy in the Stag and Pheasant that evening Pat discussed the matter. 'Well,' said Doc, 'this isn't the first time it's happened. My cab went more miles last week than I'd logged. Never ran out of diesel but it'd definitely used more than usual and it wasn't as clean as I'd left it either. You know! The usual evening litter was in there when I hadn't done any evening work.'

Billy laughed. 'You think somebody nicked it and then put it back, Doc. Be realistic, that don't happen, except on the tele.'

'No, but it's odd all the same. I opened up last week and there wasn't any sign of a break-in I could see,' replied Doc. 'Nothing missing in the office was there, Pat?'

'There's nothing to go missing in there,' replied Pat. 'The computer and stuff's locked away in that fireproof safety cabinet thing, and isn't worth nicking anyway. The only other thing I can think of is that the coffee's going down at a fair old rate.'

They parted with the vague intention of keeping an eye on things. When the complaints started coming in next day they sat up and took notice.

'Overcharging. Rudeness. Wrong address. Picking up at the road side. Cab not clean. Overloading. All the daft things you can name,' said Billy, 'and the best of it is that nobody was working at that time. It was two o'clock; we shut at midnight and the place was locked. Somebody's having a go at us!'

Trouble's a-brewing   EH

The sun may have shone for Olga but there was a storm a-brewing in another part of Trentby.

Fiona Finzy, real name Joan Gutteridge, stepped off the 11.50am from London. Ace High of Concorde Cabs had the fare to pick up and here she came: a bouncy, busty blonde all of five feet high, in five-inch heels, trailing the latest French perfume. Ace did a double take, he should be so lucky on a Wednesday morning.

'Hotel Metropole, right?' He almost saluted, old habits die hard, his handlebar moustache doing overtime as he shut down the hatch back. Wait until the rest of the flight heard about this beauty in town.

'Come for the wedding, have you?' asked Ace in his most friendly manner as he grinned his gap-toothed best below his quivering moustache. 'Big day here on Saturday, the local football derby and the local big nob's son getting hitched; guests arriving every day.'

'No, not a wedding,' she said with a gleam in her eye. 'Just looking up old friends. Who's the girl, then? I may remember her.'

'It's Yvonne Jones, the Mayor's daughter actually,' he answered, just as the intercom cut in ...

'Kilo-Alpha-Hotel. Ace to Wingco. Are you receiving me? Over.'

'Wingco to Ace. Receiving you loud and clear. After the Metropole you're in the air for The Mansions, Lady Britney needs her weekly ego massage at the health club. Over and out.'

What Wingco didn't know was that the busty blonde had heard this too and pricked up her pretty little ears. 'Lady Britney' rang a bell. Now Chummy's step-mother, interesting, she must look them up.

After her interview with the manager of the Metropole she sat in the bar and chatted to an old school chum who was the barmaid. Water had flowed under the bridge to be sure but not that much. Britney! The high school sex bomb had squirmed her way to the top of the local social circle and now was 'Lady' Britney. She needed to talk to Mum and a few more of her relatives. Aunt Vera would do for a start.

A little later one phone call to Aunty Vera confirmed the connection between Britney and the Fortesque-Chumleighs, once Vera told Bertha 'our Joanie' was back, it set the old grey matter working Bertha had a long memory for events in Trentby, Thinking back to the time before Britney became Lady Chumleigh, didn't young Chummy, in his turbulent teens, get sent away suddenly to relatives up North? Bertha's grapevine had also told her that a certain young Joannie

Gutteridge (Vera's cousin's niece) had also left town in a hurry to study 'Beauty Culture' or some such. Who had paid for that, for a kid from the wrong side of town? But as long as money was oiling the way, scandal could be avoided, and the prospective Tory MP could write it off as expenses.

The popular riverside bar at the Metropole had heard most local gossip over a friendly drink, so when Fiona Finzy slowly descended the main stairs and sashayed her way across the reception area, all eyes followed her undulations.

When one man jumped up to open the doors to the terrace, she gave him the full attention he deserved. After all wasn't she considered to be The Cleavage of the Year in the latest edition of *Beauty and the Bust?*

The wedding dress fitting   SC

The big red Number 42 bus edged its way into the town centre. There were only five people on it: two ginger-haired girls, obviously twins, with their harassed mother; an old lady with grey hair and no teeth, who burped loudly every time the bus went over a bump; and a young lady talking on her phone. She wore a large smock dress, and the way she gently rubbed her stomach it was easy to guess she was with child.

'Mam, Mam, the line's so bad I can hardly hear you. The bus is nearly there now, can you meet me outside the shop? What is that you're saying?' She was beginning to shout now as she thought that would help the connection. 'No, they can't have. Not both of them. Chicken pox *and* broken legs? This is a disaster the dresses are ready and now I have no bridesmaids. Okay, Mam, I'll see you there.'

She gently pushed the aerial down and sobbed quietly as she put the brick-like phone into a capacious bag. Somebody coughed behind her; she took no notice as she just assumed it was the old, toothless lady.

The cough came again, more loudly this time, followed by an, 'Excuse me, you seem to be having a little trouble. I couldn't help overhearing.' She turned to look at the harassed young mother. 'I might have a solution to your problem. My name is Diana Ross, not *the* Diana Ross,' she laughed nervously, 'And these are my girls, Ruby and Rosie. They were supposed to be bridesmaids for my brother but he called the wedding off when he found out his fiancée was having affairs with a plumber, a Russian diplomat and the man from Delmonte, that's the grocer's on the High Street. They were so disappointed. So if you need bridesmaids, my girls would love to do it.'

Yvonne looked at the two young faces with their bright ginger curls, blue eyes and noses liberally covered with freckles. They smiled at her pleadingly, and she made her decision.

'It would save my wedding from disaster. They look about the right size. Can you come to Madam Mordebt's right now? I'm just on my way for the final fitting. If the dresses fit you're on. What do you say girls?'

Ruby and Rosie smiled big toothy smiles and said, 'Yeah, cool!'

At that moment the bus stopped and they all trouped off, including the old lady, who started following them because she loved weddings, they always made her cry. Yvonne's mother, Janice, was waiting outside the bridal shop. When Diana saw her she grabbed the twins and curtsied deeply, 'Oh, Ma'am, I know you. Your husband is a big wig in the Council. I recognise you because I clean his office. I didn't know this was a celebrity wedding.'

Janice turned and looked at them, with a blank expression on her face.

'Sorry, Mam, this is Diana Ross, *not the Diana Ross*, and her twins Ruby and Rosie, my new bridesmaids. I don't know who the old lady is, she was on the bus and just sort of followed us.'

Gloria smiled toothlessly but didn't enlighten them. They walked into the shop as a group and Madam Mordebt swept out to meet them a broad smile on her flaccid face, her greying hair swept into a tight bun, and a silvery, silky dress covering her ample figure. When she saw them she stopped dead, the smile vanished and her face drained of colour. She eyed the bride to be up and down. 'Well, my dear you seem to have altered since your last fitting, and where are your bridesmaids? Those two charming girls.'

'They've dropped out I'm afraid, chicken pox and broken legs. These are their replacements. The dresses should fit them. I do so want a colourful wedding.' Yvonne sighed wistfully.

'Girls, your dresses are in the changing room on the left,' said Madam Mordebt, taking charge,

69

'Mother, will you help them get ready?' She turned to Yvonne, 'Your dress is on the right.'

'Thank you,' Yvonne replied, 'Mam, come on, I might need some help too.'

Madam Mordebt looked to the heavens and muttered under her breath, 'I think you'll need divine help to fit into that dress.'

Ruby and Rosie were soon ready and stepped awkwardly out of the changing room. They had bands on their heads festooned with large bright yellow flowers. The dresses were of a Mary Quant style, knee length with fluorescent red and orange squares and yellow dots liberally splashed all over. With their ginger hair and bright dresses they certainly looked, well ... colourful. Madam Mordebt looked them up and down and then declared, 'Girls, what a perfect fit. They could have been made for you.'

The old lady was still sitting observing in the corner of the room. She reached in her bag and pulled out her sunglasses. She put them on to try and soften the kaleidoscope of mismatched colours.

There came a shout from the room on the right, 'Girls, don't change back yet I want to see, but we are having a little trouble in here.'

Madam Mordebt opened the door to see Yvonne standing with a huge meringue of a dress stuck tightly around her thighs. Janice was pulling manically at it.

'I think it might need a little alteration.'

Gloria giggled as she slipped unnoticed out of the shop. This was certainly going to be a wedding to remember.

A sexy vicar?   **MH**

'No, I won't let you ... put the bottle back ... nothing good will come out of this,' begged William, as he tried unsuccessfully to seize the bottle of Jack Daniels from Trevor.

'Let me go. I will feel loads better when I ... leave me alone. Let me enjoy the moment, at last she can join me for eternity,' Trevor screamed. But the vicar was having none of it and held on to the bottle like a man possessed. Although, perhaps 'possessed' is not quite the right word.

'Come now, this is ridiculous, she never killed you did she? If you want to seek revenge surely it should be on Sir Lancelot,' suggested William calmly.

'Did I hear you say my husband's name?' Lady Britney asked, while giving the vicar a strange look as he continued to grapple with the bottle.

'Y-y-y-yes, I asked you how he was,' William stuttered.

'Oh, he's fine, I expect. He's always somewhere or another, it's hard to keep track, with the wedding and everything.'

'Good, I am pleased to hear it.'

'E-r-r-r, Vicar, I know it is a bit early, but if you want to offer me a tipple, I am quite partial to a tot of Jack Daniels now and again and again and again,' Lady Britney laughed.

'Good. I'll join in a moment,' he panted.

'Willie, shall I tell you why I want to get my revenge with her as well as that prat Lancelot? They got rid of me so they wouldn't have to share the purse when

Britney Tears won her races. Can you see why I want revenge?' Trevor stormed.

'Are you going to give me that drink or do I have to wait all morning?' Lady Britney moaned.

'Just a few moments, I have a problem holding bottles this early in the morning.'

'How long have you had a drink problem? I've never seen anyone fight a bottle before pouring a drink,' she remarked.

'Oh, you misunderstand,' he replied, because he couldn't think of anything else to say. Suddenly Trevor let go of the bottle and William went flying across the room and landed in Lady Britney's lap.

'Oh, Vicar, I didn't know you cared,' she purred sexily.

'You ought to see me in a fairy outfit,' Trevor said in an excellent imitation of William's voice.

'Vicar, you naughty boy. Like to dress up, do we?'

'Would you like a single or double,' William asked quickly.

'A double, why not? After the wedding we'll have to meet in the church. You bring your fairy outfit and I'll bring my birthday suit. It will be fun, I've never had a vicar before,' she laughed, sounding excited.

'There you go, Willie boy, you're on a promise. I have decided you're correct: it is that swine Sir Lancelot who deserves my attention,' said Trevor quietly before disappearing.

'Cheers, Vicar, here's to our rendezvous after the wedding. Can I ask you when you started drinking in the mornings?'

'I suppose about fifteen years ago, why do you

ask?'

'I just wanted to know how long it would be before I start fighting with a bottle to pour a drink. However, I needn't worry, I have a few years to go before I need to give up the booze. Bye. I think I'll look around the church.' She smiled and downed her Jack Daniels in one. 'Oh, and don't forget to bring you fairy outfit after the wedding.'

'I-I-I-I won't,' he stuttered badly as he felt himself blush.

Trentby Theatricals   MH

Ray De Wrong sat in his small office at The Trentby Theatrical Agency and wondered when the phone was going to ring. The reason why nobody wanted to hire his clients was they were all crap.

He wished he had gone to London when he had the chance. Open an agency in London they had said, more talent in London they had told him, but as a well-known know-it-all he'd ignored the advice and now he was in financial trouble.

On his books Ray had a juggler who was always dropping his props, an actor who couldn't remember lines and failed every audition he had ever attended, an opera singer who couldn't sing in Italian, a clown who was a miserable beggar, numerous mediocre dancers and singers and then there was his only band who were very good, unfortunately they played heavy metal and went by the name Death and Sunder.

Suddenly the phone rang and in his surprise he knocked it onto the floor and swore loudly. 'Hello,

Trentby Theatrical Agency. Ray speaking, how may I help you?'

'Hey, Ray, have you booked us for any gigs or arranged a tour yet?' asked Rudy Darkness, real name Jeff Smith, the lead singer of Death and Sunder.

'Rudy, mate, I am working hard for you but the recession is biting. Gigs are difficult to find.'

'I don't want to hear anymore of your excuses, either you get us some gigs or we find a new agent,' Rudy threatened.

'You know I do my best for you. Trust me, I will get you a good gig soon,' Ray promised.

'I know all about your good gigs, the last time you arranged one for us we ended up playing background music at a Women's Institute wine tasting evening,' he complained bitterly.

'Yeah, sorry about that, I thought they said Women's Gothic Society.' Ray lied easily.

'Well, this is your last chance. Find us a suitable gig or else,' Rudy told him and slammed down the phone.

Ray looked down at the pile of unpaid bills and prayed for a miracle. At that moment the phone rang again.

'Hello, Trentby Theatrical Agency. How may I help you?'

'Good morning. I'm Sir Lancelot Fortescue-Chumleigh. My son is getting married on Saturday and I require what I think is called *a pop group* to play at the reception in the evening. Do you have such a thing?'

'I have a very good group who are set for stardom.

They sing well and can play their own instruments, which is rare these days,' Ray explained

'They sound perfect. Will they be available to play this Saturday?'

'They are very busy. Let me find out if I can fit you in.'

Ray paused for a moment and rustled some papers close to the phone's mouth piece. 'Sir Lancelot you are in luck, I can fit you into their schedule.'

'Splendid, splendid, how much will they cost?'

'Well, they are fairly well known so that increases their fee. How does fifteen hundred pounds sound as a special deal?' he said, crossing his fingers for luck.

'Fine, more than I wanted to pay but, hey-ho, it is my son's wedding after all.'

'Thank you for booking them. Could you leave me a deposit?' Ray asked hopefully.

'Of course, I will send one of my people around with a cheque,' Sir Lancelot agreed.

'Made out to cash. I have to pay the band before they appear,' he lied again.

'Well, if that is the way it's done, so be it. Good day to you, sir.'

Ray replaced the receiver and jumped for joy, before phoning Rudy Darkness to tell him the good news - but not the venue.

How does it go together?   SMS

'Hey up, our Vera,' wheezed Gloria, struggling up the steps carrying two large cardboard boxes. 'Lazy beggar that young Wyatt, wouldn't carry these in for me, said his knee was giving him gip.'

From the window Vera watched the rear lights of the Cavalry Cab disappear round the corner by the recycling bins and was just in time to see the tail of something long and pink scurry into the bottle bank.

'Is that the ...?' asked Vera gleefully wielding the scissors ready to cut the sticky tape.

'Yep. One chocolate fountain kit as requested!' beamed Gloria, the circles on her cheeks glowing the same cerise colour as her cupid-bow lipstick, 'and on the step is a very big catering-sized jar of gherkins, very popular at bar mitzvahs apparently, and all the white chocolate they had in the cash and carry on Elm Street. I won't get the raw berries until Saturday morning or they'll go off. Here's the receipts. Our Gwen wouldn't take a penny, bless her heart.'

'Oh, don't leave all that chocolate out there, it'll attract rats,' said Vera, rushing towards the door to assist her cousin. Just at that moment the phone rang.

'He-llo, Lady Vee, your Goddess of the Morning. How may I help you into paradise? An escort? For Saturday afternoon? Yes, that's not a problem for Trentby Discreet Escort Services. We have a variety of ... Oh, you know who you want to book. Right, I'll see if your choice is free of engagement! Olga. You want Olga. And what is the event? The Mayor's daughter's wedding! You want to book one of our girls as an escort for you as a guest at the Mayor's daughter's wedding?'

Gloria, who was at that moment carrying in the jar

of gherkins stood speechless in the doorway. Her jaw dropped open. 'Who is it?' she mouthed wordlessly.

'Righto, Inspector Mackay. That's noted in the appointment book. Good morning.'

'Bertha will do her nut,' said Gloria but before she could elaborate further the phone rang again.

'He-llo, Lady Vee, your Goddess of the Morning. How can I help you into paradise? Oh, hello, Squadron Leader. Yes, I did ask Bertha about your suggestion but no, emphatically no, dear. Trentby Discreet Phone-in Services will not be offering "Frequent Flyer" miles. Are you alright, dear? You sound a bit croaky. You haven't pranged your kite again, have you? Oh, you have! Plastered up to the thigh, laid up on the sofa for a while.'

Gloria wasn't listening, she was too busy sampling one of the chocolate bars from the stack of boxes she had just heaved up the steps.

It was quite apt, though, thought Gloria, knowing the client's proclivities. Vera was again unwrapping another sample with one hand, as she fiddled with the CD player with the other. 'Okay, are we ready for action? Whipped cream and chocolate sauce bottles loaded and primed? Wait for it! Wait for it! The Dam Busters are taking off and it's chocs away, Squadron Leader, chocs away.'

De Wrong gets sacked MH

Ray De Wrong opened the door to his office and ran up the stairs with his lunch and a full wallet. He smiled as he opened it and pulled out fifteen hundred pounds.

'Right then five hundred pounds for Death and Sunder, that leaves a thousand for me. Pay the rent two hundred, the phone one hundred a fifty, one hundred in petty cash. That leaves me five fifty,' he said out loud.

'Hello, Ray. Couldn't help but overhear you,' said Rudy Darkness from the top of the stairs.

'What do you want?' Ray replied nervously while trying to make the piles of money disappear.

'You cheating us again, Ray? I told you what would happen if you did,' Rudy said menacingly.

'I can explain everything. I made a mistake, there is six hundred for you, and I would never cheat you,' he said, as his voice seemed to rise an octave or two.

'Hey, Vamp, come here and listen to Jacko and his bullshit,' he said to his cousin twice removed on his mother's side whose real name was Cecil Twonk, the drummer in the band, who was also bouncer at the local nightclub and build like a brick outhouse.

'What's going on? Is he cheating us again?' Vamp asked in his slow monotone voice.

'Keeping more money than he should, doing us out of what is rightly ours,' Rudy replied.

'Shall I have a quiet word in his ear, eh, Rudy?' breathed Vamp.

'N-n-n-no, there is no need for violence. Look seven hundred pounds that is my last offer,' Ray said shakily.

'How much is your commission? I understood it was twenty per cent, if my memory serves. Now I was never very good at maths at school but it occurs to me that your payment is three hundred quid not a thousand you no good son of a bitch,' Rudy shouted while throwing two fifty, and ten twenty, pound notes at Ray.

'I need the money! Otherwise I'll have to close down the agency,' Ray threatened.

'Let it close, because from this moment on you are no longer representing Death and Sunder. After this gig on Saturday we are moving down to London, where we will find an agent who will get us into the limelight so our music can be heard around the world,' Rudy smiled.

'Don't hold your breath, Rudy. You'll never be a headliner,' Ray said snidely.

'At least we will have a chance to try; whereas you have tried and failed miserably,' Rudy replied sarcastically.

'Enjoy your gig at the Labour Club. I would like to bet it's your last.'

Ray laughed as the door banged shut.

Mrs Richardson strikes back   JP

'Taxi, darlin'?'

As the Concorde Cab screeched to a halt on the zebra crossing, Mrs Richardson leapt smartly back on to the pavement, or at least as smartly as a 79-year-old with two baskets of Tesco groceries could leap. She'd planned on walking to the bus station but she was already getting out of puff and it had started to rain. She might as well take advantage, she thought. 'Thank you, young man. Could you give me a hand with my shopping?'

'Not me, darlin'. Not with my back,' said Derek Dodd. 'Doctor says if I lift anything heavier than a pint of Trentby Bitter, it's odds on I'll never walk again. Now you wouldn't want that on your conscience, would you?'

'I suppose not,' said Mrs Richardson, sliding her baskets on to the back seat. She settled herself in and closed the door. 'King Edward Avenue, please. Number 22.'

'That'll be ten quid, darlin',' said Derek.

'Ten pounds? That nice Bobby Owen only charged me four pounds last month,' said Mrs Richardson, not certain how much money she'd got left in her purse.

'Last month, you say? Well, that explains it. Last month was summer. Now it's winter and the new European Union Taxi Directive comes in. Higher fares in winter 'cos it costs more to run the taxis, see. Lights and heater are on longer. You know how it is yourself.'

'But it's only September,' protested Mrs Richardson. 'It's not winter until November.'

'Oh, I grant you the English winter starts in November but we're talking Europe here. It's down to where they put the international date thingy. You're lucky I stopped for you when I did. There's a two- pound surcharge after six o'clock.' Mrs Richardson looked at the clock on the dashboard: five minutes to six. 'Ten pounds, you said?'

'That's right, darlin'. Call it twelve with the standard twenty per cent service charge that's been agreed throughout Europe from the first of September on account of how helpful we cabbies are.'

'But aren't you supposed to wait and charge what it says on that thing when we get there?' asked Mrs Richardson, pointing to the fare meter above the windscreen. 'Normally, yes,' explained Derek, 'but with all this new pricing we're waiting for the new meters from Brussels. They've sent them out by taxi but they haven't arrived yet.'

'Have you got any change?' asked a bemused Mrs Richardson. 'I've only got fifteen pounds.'

'Sorry, darlin'. Just banked all me change before I picked you up. Give us the fifteen quid and whichever of the lads picks you up next time'll knock three quid off. Can't say fairer than that, can I?' Mrs Richardson handed over the notes and wished she'd braved the rain.

When they arrived in King Edward Avenue, Mrs Richardson didn't know where she'd left her stomach. She'd been thrown backwards and forwards, left and right, not to mention up and down over the speed bumps in Jordan Road. She'd seen at least one red light flash by, lost count of the number of times they'd hit the kerb and, with the abuse other drivers had shouted at Derek, her vocabulary had increased considerably.

'Here we are, darlin', grinned Derek, 'Quick as you can, now.' Mrs Richardson opened the door and cautiously swung both legs out of the car, stopping at the last moment to get some leverage from the door handle. Derek didn't expect a delay and let out the clutch. Mrs Richardson fell back onto the seat, legs in the air and most of next week's washing on display.

When Derek had slapped on the brakes, she pulled herself up. If the Incredible Hulk had seen the look on her face he'd have found it much easier to play the role. She was livid. It wasn't that she'd never had her legs that high before. She had, but that was between her and her late departed Dickie. This was different. No one could subject Jemima Richardson to such indignity and get away with it. She picked up a two-pound bag of Homepride flour from the top of her basket and smashed it over Derek's head. 'Take that, you f-f-flippin' crook,' she yelled.

Derek stumbled out of the cab, shaking his white head like a demented dervish. Then he suddenly realized his feet were leaving the ground, up and up he went. Was this why it was called self-raising flour, he thought. Derek's questionable grasp of the law of gravity didn't last long. What goes up must come down and he hit the bonnet of the taxi with a sickening thud before rolling onto the drive by the passenger door. Without looking back he scrambled to his feet and ran down the road followed by a billowing white cloud.

'Bobby, am I glad to see you,' sighed Mrs Richardson, 'but what are you doing here?'

'I finished early today so I thought I'd pop round. See if you needed anything.' Bobby Owen, one of Concorde Cab's regular drivers, finished dusting himself down and helped get the shopping out of the cab. 'How come a nice lady like you crowns matey with a bag of self-raisin'?' Mrs Richardson told Bobby what had happened.

'It's not like Mr Miller to take on a driver like that,

Bobby,' she said.

'Oh, he's not one of our drivers. There's been some funny business going on these last few days. This is Ace's cab. It was nicked from outside his flat last night.'

'What's that, Bobby?' asked Mrs Richardson as she picked up a jar of Branston Pickle from the drive-way. 'By the front wheel. Looks like a wallet.'

'It must have fell out of matey's pocket in his rush to leave us,' said Bobby, opening the pouch. His name's Derek Dodd and he's left us his address as well. You weren't the only one he ripped off today by the look of the cash in here.' Bobby handed her a crisp twenty-pound note. 'Put this in your purse, Mrs Richardson. It'll cover your fare and your bag of self-raisin'. Now let's get you inside and make a nice cup of tea. I'll take Ace's cab back later.'

'Thanks, Bobby. Do you know where to take it?' asked Mrs Richardson.

'Oh, I know where to take it all right,' said Bobby, giving her a cheeky wink.

Wednesday evening   JP

'Where's that useless pillock got to?' Dave Dodd muttered.

He switched off the TV in his brother's flat. Derek had said on the phone he'd just do a few more pick-ups and then he'd be straight home but Dave had already been there long enough to watch some ghosts-and-ghouls rubbish. All he wanted was his share of the day's takings before he headed off to

The Fokkers Arms, down by Trentby International Airport. The pub was rather too modern for Dave's liking but the trolley-dollies staying over night in Trentby always made it their first stop. All flash and plastic, Dave thought - but they were good company.

'At last!' sighed Dave as the street door banged. He reached to open the door into the dim passageway that led to the front of the house, ready to give Derek a piece of his mind. 'Aaarrrghhh!' he screamed as he came face-to-face with a ghostly apparition. He fell to the floor, tucking his head in to make a ball and, as he rolled around the passageway, began to chant: 'Holy Mary, Mother of God, pray for us sinners ...' Dave wasn't a Catholic; that was what the guy being chased by ghouls in the film had done. He'd survived and ended up in bed with a statuesque Swedish blonde, so it was worth a try, reasoned Dave.

'What the chuffing hell's wrong with you, you big Jessie?' laughed the apparition.

'Derek ... is that you?' sniffled Dave as he risked opening one eye to peer at his brother. 'What happened to your face?'

'Oh, just had a difference of opinion with some old dear and a bag of self-raisin'. The bad news is: I lost me wallet.'

'Don't tell me the takings were in there. What am I going to do for spends down The Fokkers?'

'I don't think you'll be going boozin' tonight. Me address was in there as well. As soon as that old lady and her mate find it, the coppers'll be round here in no time.'

'Right,' said Dave, 'get yerself cleaned up and

pack a bag. I'll nip home for some cash and be back here in half an hour. We'll drive to Liverpool and catch the ferry to the Isle of Man. We can stay with old Charlie Smithers 'till the coppers have found the cabs. When they see there's no harm done, they'll move on to something else and it'll be safe for us to come back.'

'But it could take 'em ages to find the cabs,'

'Not if we give 'em a clue,' chuckled Dave.

Elsewhere on Wednesday evening   EH

With Jim out at a Rotary Club 'Men Only' do, Janice, his long suffering Mayoress and partner, looked forward to an evening alone; or almost alone as she never knew when her daughter, the bride-to-be, Yvonne, would come walking in. But it was the phone that intruded.

'Hello, who is it?' she said resignedly. 'What's up Wyatt? Speak slower, yer daft idiot ... Yes, I got that bit about your mate's let you down. Which mate, and what's he done?'

There was a short silence broken by Wyatt's quick breathing, then, 'Sorry Jan, it's not my fault the axle broke. The damned carriage hasn't been moved in ages.' The silence this time was longer ...

'Wyatt, get your mind in gear, you've got to do something! Our Yvonne's in enough of a state already,' she could hear his wheezing breath clearly now.

Then at last he said, 'I've got another mate in Lichfield, has a white limo, he might help.'

'That's not white horses, is it? She's set her

heart on white horses and jingly bells!' As she slammed the phone down the door bell rang.

What now? Her quiet evening was ruined!

Later Wednesday evening   JP

'What the blood and stomach pills is he doin'?' chuntered Biggles as he signalled a left turn into Barbara Castle Mews.

The ageing hippy stepped into the road towards him oblivious to the blast on the horn of Ace's cab that had been doctored to mimic an RAF scramble siren.

He hadn't been counting on having to relocate Ace's cab that evening, Once he'd checked on Mrs Richardson he'd planned to knock off for the day. As usual on a Wednesday, the Trentby International Chippy had a tray of chicken tikka meat and chips - with a healthy salad - that had his name on it. But he'd got through the Trentby rush hour surprisingly quickly and come off the roundabout just in time to see the joker he now knew from the dropped wallet to be Derek Dodd, driving away with some other guy at a rate of knots. Now this long-haired twonk was in his way. 'Twonk!' shouted Biggles in frustration through the open window.

Long Hair stopped by the side of the cab and Biggles wished he'd held his tongue. He was younger and much larger than he'd seemed across the road.

'Yes?' he said through the window.

'Didn't you hear the horn?' asked Biggles.

'Why d'you want to know when I was born?'

'Why would I want to know when you were born?'

asked Biggles.

'Well, you know my name.'

'I don't know your name. I said you were a twonk.'

'I know,' explained Long Hair unzipping his jacket to reveal a T-shirt sporting a picture of his much-younger self and the caption 'Cecil Twonk, legendary drummer with Death and Sunder'. 'Trouble is the old hearing's not as good as it was.'

'Bit of a drawback for a musician, isn't it?' sympathised Biggles.

'Not really,' explained Cecil, 'I can feel the beat through the floor and to be honest it can be a blessing not hearing the bloody racket night after night.'

'I know what you mean,' laughed Biggles, 'I'm a Glen Miller fan myself. Nice to meet you anyway, Cecil. You keep your eyes peeled on these roads.' As Cecil walked off, Biggles thought he'd better review some of his driving vocabulary. What was the likelihood of meeting a Trentby pedestrian rejoicing in the name of Pillock?

'That should do it,' he muttered as he drew the taxi on to the pavement outside the door of the Dodds' flat, 'Let's see how long it takes Trentby's Finest to find that.'

THURSDAY

Give us a clue   JP

'You've got a what for me?' growled Mackay, 'a co-nundrum ... a bleedin' conundrum? I'm a police inspector not Hercule Bleedin' Parrot.'

Chris Cross hadn't expected this reaction when he called to give Inspector Bruce Wallace Mackay the letter that had arrived at the *Trentby Evening News* that morning. He had thought a thank-you and a bit of an exclusive might come his way but if you were head of vice, senior CID officer and acting head of what Mackay himself affectionately called the wooden-tops when referring to Trentby's uniformed force, it was understandable if life sometimes got a little fraught.

'Well, hand it over, then,' sighed Mackay. He took a pair of tweezers from his desk to extract the single sheet of blue notepaper from the matching envelope Chris placed in front of him.

'It's from the Isle of Man,' said Chris.

'Oh? What makes you think that?'

'Well, the postmark on the envel...' Chris held his breath as soon as he realised from the glare on Mackay's face that finishing this statement of the obvious would mean he'd be back covering weddings and WI outings as soon as Mackay could phone his editor.

The Inspector's eyes slowly returned to the letter: 'A copper in Trentby's looking for taxis. They're all at sea. So stop for tea. Then go to hell. Where are they? Can you tell? Hardly William bleedin' Wordsworth, is it?

'No, but I thought ...' began Chris.

'We'll do the thinking, thank you, Mr Cross. That's the trouble with you lot. You think policing's a game; as easy as ABC. Well, I can tell you, it bleedin' well isn't. It's hard slog, laddie. Hard bleedin' slog.'

'I know, but ...'

'That'll be all, Mr Cross. You'll hear from us when we're ready to make a statement to the press.'

Chris closed the office door behind him and made his way out of the police station. 'As easy as ABC,' he muttered. 'I wonder if ...'

Metropole foyer gossip   EH

'Seen the blonde waiting for the taxi? She'll set tongues wagging at the Health Club all right. She's got an interview, I heard, for the new Beauty Bar they're opening.'

The receptionist at the Metropole knew all the gossip, kept up to date by her boyfriend, a part-time driver with Cavalry Cabs. 'She calls herself Fiona Finzy now,' said Gina to her mate. 'They say she used to live over the chip shop in Railway Terrace with her mam and gran.'

'Yeah, I remember her at school, always boasting about her absent father; but Bertha says to my gran she was one of Lord FC's mistakes, and Bertha knows what that means,' and off went the two of them behind the office door to have a great giggle.

Ace High of Concorde Cabs was in luck again. 'Health Club is it, darlin'?' and his eyes swivelled dangerously around to see the length of thigh near his left hand.

'Thanks, yes,' said Fiona, 'you'll be seeing a lot more of me soon,' giving him a sidelong glance. Ace felt the sweat from his hand on the steering wheel. What did she mean? he pondered, as she wriggled her curves into the passenger seat next to him.

One of our cabs is missing   CMH

'Dusty! Did Number 15 have an accident after I left last night?' queried Ginger. 'It's not in the yard and there's no sign of it in the garage.'

Dusty turned to the logbook. 'Nothing on the log and I'm sure the evening crew would have said something,' he replied. 'Not due for a service for another couple of hundred miles anyway. Are you sure you didn't take it home with you?'

'Dead positive! I was going to give it a quick run through the car wash first thing this morning and then go on the school run. What the devil's happened to it now?'

'Gone walkabout I would guess. Did you leave the keys in it?'

'What do you take me for, Dusty? A chuffing clown or something?' Resignedly he ticked the points off on his fingers. 'In the garage, check! Doors locked, check! Windows shut, check! Keys in the key safe, check! All as routine orders. It's been nicked again, but they won't get far this time; it was almost out of diesel. There was only about thirty miles in the tank. Nothing else for it, I'll have to go round and see the Plod. You never know they might have some clue

They did.

'Yes, we know exactly were it is, what's left of it anyway,' was the answer he got. 'You must have seriously hacked off whoever nicked it last night. It took twenty minutes for the fire crew to douse the flames from the explosion,' he was told. 'The kids' area of Hammer Park will have to be rebuilt and the council will be knocking on your door for the insurance details. Here's the crime number to give them so that we can do the necessary.'

Cursing furiously all the way, Ginger returned to the office.

'That's that, then,' was Dusty's remark. 'You'll have to claim on your insurance for the cab and loss of earnings. As soon as you've done that, get the spare out and do the uphill run. The Heights to St. Mary's first, then there's a 9.45 pick-up, a Miss Finzie it says here, at 16 Trentside Way for the hairdresser's.' Dusty threw him the keys.

Two minutes later Ginger was back in the office asking, 'Where's the spare, Dusty?' Seeing the blank look on Dusty's face he collapsed into a chair and burst into furious tears repeating the litany, 'I'll get them, I will. I'll get them!'

Ordering flowers   EJW

Tarquine was fluttering around the shop, filling vases with water and arranging flowers in types and colours.

He was happy, humming to himself as he worked. He was in a new relationship. It had been some time since he had been in love. His last affair had taken its toll and a long time to recover from. His lover had decided to try to enter into politics, like his father, resulting in him needing to clean up his act. Getting involved with a lady seemed the only way he thought it could be done.

He was heartbroken at the time, but life was made good again when he met his new love at a cross-dressing party. Not really his scene but some-times you could be lucky to find a one-night stand with no ties; he had found his naughty-fairy, Tinker-bell - Tinkers for short. Their platonic affair began, upon the insistence of Tinkers; only discreet meet-ings at Tarquine's house were agreed, with personal everyday life a no-go area. Tinkers sometimes acted strangely, especially at meal times when he insisted on saying grace and blessing the bread and wine. Tarquine was happy with the arrangement but lived in hope that they would eventually become lovers. Tarquine enjoyed the cross-dressing as much as Tinkers and provided many new outfits for their en-joyment.

The telephone shrilled bringing Tarquine out of his day dreaming.

'Good morning, Daisy Chain florists, Tarquine speaking. How can I help you?'

'Oh, good morning, Tarquine. I'm Janice Jones, the Mayoress, you may have heard of me.' Janice purred assuming the soft-woman approach would be useful. 'I have a problem which requires urgent attention.

My daughter's getting married on Saturday, a rush job you understand. We have only just realised that no flowers have been ordered. Can you possibly accommodate us?'

Tarquine gulped, 'This Saturday is rather short notice, I shall have to check my order book, I'm very busy,' he lied, visualising the extra charges he could make for the emergency. He only had one other order, a funeral, which could be made up later that day. Flowers were always second rate for funerals, no one ever looked at them properly, they were always too upset.

'Emm, I can fit you in at a cost. You see I will have to employ more help with the arranging. That depends on your requirements, Ma'am.'

Janice was distressed, this was the last florist in the *Yellow Pages*. All the others were too busy. She pleaded, 'Oh Tarquine, please help us. My daughter is pregnant as you have probably guessed but she is marrying into a very respectable family and as Mayoress I can put a lot of work your way. We have lots of dinners, dances and banquets that need flowers.'

Tarquine smiled to himself, how could he refuse that offer? 'Well, Madam Mayoress, or can I call you Janice? Let me see what I can do. I need lots of details but first let's start with the bride and groom's names.'

Janice breathed a sigh of relief, 'Thank you so much, I will not forget your kindness. My daughter's name is Yvonne, and the groom's name is The Honourable Jason Fortescue-Chumleigh.'

Tarquine felt his pulse-rate quicken with sudden

heat spreading from his neck upwards. He stuttered, the word REVENGE flashing before his eyes, 'Oh Janice, I have a feeling this is going to be one of the best weddings I have ever arranged flowers for.'

New cabs for old   CMH

As usual the newly opened First Class International Lounge at Trentby Airport was deserted, the light refreshment kiosk closed and the news-stands empty. The only person in sight being a cleaner, leaning on the same lackadaisical mop that she'd leaned on for the last month, and with as much result.

The door from the Customs and Excise office opened and head poked out saying, 'International private flight inbound, Annabel. You'd better get the kettle on,' and then disappeared like a turtle into her shell.

'Hell's teeth,' Annabel muttered. 'That means getting stuff out and opening the till. Just when I wanted to get off early. Ohh well!' She went around switching on lights and display boards, eventually ending up opening the shutters to the light refreshment kiosk to await her very first customers.

'Two latte, light on the sugar, heavy on the cream, honey,' said a transatlantic voice as Annabel was peering into the dark space under her counter wondering where she'd put that silly hat she was supposed to wear.

Pasting a smile on her face she looked up into an overeager face with a smile as big as a bucket. 'Certainly, sir. If you'd like to take a seat I'll bring them over when they're percolated.'

'Gee, I love that English accent,' said the face as it disappeared.

Carefully pulling the handles and smelling the fragrant steam she looked at her first customer. *Yank,* she thought. *Not overweight. Looks fit and wearing good clothes. Must be well off to come in on a private flight. Probably ...* here her thoughts were disrupted as the coffee machine gave its final 'Bluuurp splat' and stopped. 'Mocha was it, sir?' she asked her lonely customer.

'Yep, one for me an' th' other for my cousin th' Honourable Jason Fortesque-Chumleigh when he gets here. I guess he won't be long 'cos I phoned him when we got into British airspace. It'll take a while for your baggage handlers to unload my stuff.'

'That will be three pounds twenty, please sir,' she said as she placed the cups and saucers down on the table in front of him, following them with the cream jug and sugar basin. 'I thought you'd like to add your own cream and sugar. Then it must be just right, mustn't it?'

'How much is that in real money, honey?' he asked with a smile.

'About five dollars and fifty cents,' was the reply.

'Is that all, and for special service as well? I don't have any pounds yet so here's twenty dollars; that should cover it, I guess.' At that moment the entry doors opened and Jason walked through.

'Hi, Jason. How they hangin'?' said the traveller as the pair smiled and shook hands.

'Mornin', Wytch. Hi, Annabel,' Jason greeted the

pair. 'I see you've met my cousin Wytch, then, Annabel. This is Annabel Lloyd; we used to go to infant school together, but she's grown up a little since then.'

'So've you, Jason, so've you,' was the smiling reply. 'But I must get on with my job. Thanks for the tip Wytch. I hope we'll meet again.'

'Probably at my wedding on Saturday,' said Jason. 'Your father did get the invite, didn't he?'

'Mum and Dad will be there, but there's no rest for the wicked you know. I'll be stuck here until about three but I'll make the reception, almost wearing my best party frock as Dad would say.' Annabel pointed to a baggage handler beckoning through the window. 'Looks as if your luggage is ready.'

As the men turned to go Jason asked, 'Where's Avis?'

'LA last time I heard. That was after the divorce, with her new lover, I'd guess.'

'Oh, sorry, W3, I didn't know.'

'Nothin' to be sorry about, Jason. One of them things you know. She took me for twenty million at the divorce but I'm glad she's gone. Turned out she only married me for the money anyway!'

Jason laughed, 'Serves you right for being rich! Come on, let's get you sorted out and then we can have a chin-wag.'

'Got you a coffee here, Jason; there's no rush, my bags will be ready when I call for them.'

'So how was the flight?'

'Nothin' unusual. A little side wind over the Med and bumpy over the Alps but that's about all. You got me a good room?'

'Yes, you're staying with us again. In the same room as last time'

'Now who's this Yvonne Jones you're marrying? Daughter of the local mayor you said, you going into politics, old buddy?'

'No. Well, not straight away anyhow; just into the taxi, sorry, cab, business. I'm trying to buy a cab firm that recently went belly-up and run it. Not a word to anyone, even Dad. It's hush-hush at present.'

'How much do you need, buddy? I mean, it can't be a whole lot for a busted firm, can it? And how soon can you get running. Always a big deal that.'

'If I can get £160,000, it's all ready to go. I can be running in twelve hours.'

'Is that all! Chump change is that. Right let's go down to your lawyer's office and get the deal done. Call it a wedding present to your new wife if you like. I get 51%, your Yvonne Jones gets 40%, and you get the rest — and all the fun of running it. Deal?'

They shook hands. 'Deal,' they both said; both totally unaware of the consequences.

Entertainment?   ACW

'Good morning. Tim Appledore Entertainments,' answered the owner and sole office-bod, on his first call for an age.

'Hello. I'm Jim Jones, the Mayor of Trentby. This Saturday evening, entertainment is required at the clubhouse of Trentby Golf Club. I'll not be having any nonsense fees, so don't waste my time. Affordable and good quality is what is sought, Okay!'

Tim thought, *Oh why don't you have your cake and eat it. You get what you pay for in life,* but said aloud in his best sales patter, 'Indeed so, Mr Jones. Best value is our company motto.'

'We'll see. I thought about the Spanish Mariachoes from Mexico?'

'Ah, excellent choice. You've heard of the Mari Achoe troupe, then? They offer a special discount for first-time customers. I'll see if they're free this Saturday.'

Tim shuffled some of his many final demand invoices piled high on his desk.

'Ah yes, you're in luck. They are available this Saturday. There is a 10% reservation deposit required by cheque, made out to cash.'

'Righto. I'll have the cheque delivered by hand as me secretary goes up by you on her way home to the village.'

'Ah yes,' said Tim quick-thinking, so as not to expose the fact that his office was a little timber chalet behind his old miner's brick cottage. 'You'll be able to drop it off in my secure post box at the end of my office drive. Your invoice will be there in a plastic transit envelope awaiting your secretary. Thank you for choosing Tim Appledore Entertainments. Goodbye, Mr Jones.'

Tim wrote the details of the booking in his ledger, bare of any other bookings at all for his few signed-up acts, for many a day now. *Hope this breaks my run of bad luck or I'll soon have to do a midnight flit away from me debts,* thought Tim.

'Right,' said Tim to himself, 'Booking Saturday evening. Mari Achoe's Macabre Theatre troupe, Plumed Serpent of Death.'

'Ah, good, we finally have a booking out of you.'

'Oh, Manuel, I didn't hear you come in. Yes. Yes, this Saturday, too.'

Manuel Montezuma was a huge bulk of sulky Aztec, a native Mexican, who had a heavily pregnant wife and five kids to support, as well as keeping happy a whole theatre troupe of cousins who also had large families back home in Mexico to look after. But all had not gone well in past gigs: the actress with one singed eyebrow; the prop that came to life in a cloud of enraged wasps; and the famous one where the plumed serpent started swearing in high pitched Aztec shrieks as part of his anatomy became snagged in the beast's wire frame, snaring all that he held dear.

Manuel took his copy of the invoice booking from Tim and studied it, observing, 'Ah, a posh country club.'

'Yes, the golf clubhouse has a large terrace and lawns behind it with solar lights.'

'Excellent. Dim lighting to add to the ambience, with under-lit faces to add to the horror of the play, with the hypnotic trance music playing to lull and add to the terror when the damned victims scream.'
Oh yeah, what a laugh a minute that'll be, thought Tim.

Tango at the tills   CMH

'Would you like a cup of coffee, Mr Miller? The manager may be a few minutes, she's just popped into the cloakroom.' Coming from what Dusty would charitably call a 'homely' secretary this sounded as if the wait could be long.

'Erm … No, thanks,' was the reply. 'Could you tell me, is she usually in the Ladies for a long time?'

'Oh no, never more than three or four minutes. Mrs Warmsley will be out shortly.' She went back to bashing her keyboard.

The door opened and a gaunt figure under a strict hairdo came through. 'Would you like to come into my office, Mr Miller?' Although phrased as a request it was an order.

'Now, Mr Miller! About your account. As part of routine checks we go over our smaller business accounts on a regular basis. Your account has several odd features to it, but let us start at the beginning, shall we?

'For a start, the incoming cash flow is very erratic, startlingly erratic according to our experts. Then there are certain routine payments that don't appear to have been met: income tax, national insurance, employer's liability insurance and similar things. Wages also don't appear to have been paid for the last few months. Should the tax people ask the question, do you have an answer, Mr Miller?'

Dusty had been prepared for this one. 'Yes! In fact, it's all very simple: my drivers are all self-employed. This, of course, means that I, that is Concorde, don't pay many of those taxes. All I do is provide an umbrella service for them, for which they pay me.

'Concorde doesn't own very much, just the office furniture, a spare cab and a few other odds and ends. The premises are rented, at a peppercorn rent

I may add, from the old Locksley Company. The last annual accounts highlighted a satisfactory state of affairs; however, I thought you may ask about it so I've brought you a copy.' He took out a very thin document from the battered carrier bag that did duty as his briefcase and passed it across the desk.

'But while I'm here I want to talk to you about a substantial loan to grow the business. As you know, Trentby Weddings have gone out of business and I, that is Concorde, would like to take over all, or part, of their operation. I'm preparing some rough figures of my idea of the true worth of the Trentby Weddings business. Regrettably, there just hasn't been time to have them prepared for formal discussion. Essentially, of course, it's up to the liquidators: have you heard who they are, by the way?'

Mrs Warmsley did not look impressed. 'Mr Miller, it is no secret that this bank has a substantial holding in that company and will be looking very carefully,' she managed to make those two words seem threatening, 'at anyone who offers to buy the business. I'll arrange another interview for next week after I've looked, very carefully, at your figures. This will give you time to put your proposal in writing, won't it?'

Dusty had to agree that it would be satisfactory and left the office feeling wrung out.

'Exorcisms Are Us'   MH

'Thanks for persuading me not to upset Lady Britney, the wedding on Saturday will be the perfect time. By the time I have finished with Sir Lancelot's family my vengeance will be complete,' Trevor laughed uncontrollably.

'No, Trevor, it's time you gave up your insane need to exact revenge on the Fortescue-Chumleigh family,' William told him crossly.

'Oh, and what are you going to do to stop me, Willie boy? What you are going to do is nothing, because there is nothing you can do. So you might as well butt out. Saturday will be a day to remember for the Church of the Bleeding Heart, a day when the entire population of dear old Trentby will remember when Trevor the poltergeist destroyed Sir Lancelot and his family. The day when I will get the revenge I so richly deserve.'

'Trevor, I have a better idea, why don't you tell me where you lay buried and I can go to the police and tell them where you are?'

'No, William, that won't do. I found a watery grave, and Lancelot has too many contacts. He will find a way to worm his way out of any blame for my death, trust me my way is the best way.'

'Good luck to you, Trevor, I don't think there is anything I can do or say to make you change your mind. So I will say goodbye,' William said sadly.

'Won't I see you on Saturday so you can witness my retribution?

'No, I don't think so. Goodbye, Trevor, I do hope you change your mind,' William walked out of the church. He quickly walked to the vicarage and without speaking to his wife went straight to the study, onto the Internet and he typed the word 'exorcism'.

Almost instantly the screen lit up with the heading *'Exorcism by the Experts'.*

William immediately pressed the button and a big advert flashed across the screen.

'Have you a ghastly ghoul? Does your ghost get you hot and bothered? Have you a putrid poltergeist polluting your house? If the answer to any of these questions is yes, then phone Exorcism's Are Us or contact us via our website. Our rates are competitive and for a short time only we are offering easy payment terms, along with a special offer of buy one exorcism, get another free. Contact us now! You know it makes sense!'

William immediately composed an email to them and waited for a reply. While he sat waiting he wished he had a drink, so he went into the kitchen and poured himself a cup of strong coffee. He needed something stronger but his wife had cleared the house of alcohol, so caffeine would have to do.

As he entered his study he saw he had a reply to his email.

'Hey, this wouldn't be the Reverend William Warmer at the Church of the Bleeding Heart ,would it? This is Julian Hogg, your old pal from Uni. I own Exorcism's Are Us. What can I do for you, my old mate?'

William looked at the ceiling and shook his head in disgust because he hated the man, but he still decided to reply.

Dublin flashback   KD

Chummy and Tom met for a drink at the Bull. Soon their conversation turned to reminiscences of the stag weekend two weeks ago. Tom was in top form.

'It was a great party, Chummy. There we was: you, me, Charlie, Chris, Barry, Daniel and Jack on the Dublin plane that Friday,' he said, counting them off on his fingers.

Chummy's eyes misted over as the lost weekend flashed before his eyes. Chummy's stag weekend had come around so fast, for it was only two months ago it had been planned. Jason and his half-brother, Tom, who was his best man, were to meet Charlie, Chris, Craig, Barry, Daniel and Jack, the rest of the gang, at the airport: they were off to Dublin.

A Concorde taxi picked Jason and Tom up that Friday evening at six o'clock, they were flying at eight o'clock. It was only a fifteen-minute drive to the airport. At the terminal the gang were waiting impatiently for they were so excited. They couldn't wait for the fun and games to begin. Jason jumped out of the taxi, leaving Tom to pay the man.

All the lads had rucksacks so they didn't have to wait for luggage once at their destination. Having booked in by half past six, it was time for the lads to just sit and chill with a beer or two. The flight was actually on time. The lads boarded the aeroplane and found their seats, each taking a good look around at the other passengers. Jack then realised he was sat at the side of a newly reformed Irish boy band.

Jack, who wasn't a great fan of the popular group,

then thought about how much his girlfriend Kayley was into them and here was an opportunity for him to get their autographs for her. As he did, Craig pulled out his camera to take several photographs.

Forty minutes later, they were in Dublin catching a bus into the city centre. The hotel was situated in the middle of the shops, bars, restaurants and night-clubs. They arrived at ten past nine, where they booked into the hotel and went up to their rooms, in twos, Chris and Craig, Charlie and Daniel, Barry and Jack and, last but not least, Chummy and Tom.

Chummy and Tom's room was a deluxe suite with a Jacuzzi and a balcony. The other rooms were just basic standard. They all met up in Chummy and Tom's room ten minutes later, with each of them well impressed with what they were presented with once through the door. There were eight cans of Stella lager in the fridge and a little note from the manager saying, 'Hoping you have the brilliant weekend. Best wishes, Sean'. With that, the lads had their cans in the Jacuzzi, and as not one of them had brought their trunks, they were splashing about stark naked.

After the nice relaxing Jacuzzi, Jason's mates pinned him down and covered his legs, underarms and every hair on his body in toothpaste, then shaved it off. As he squealed they covered him in moisturiser and a fake tan. Not content, they forced on a pair of pink panties followed by a bra stuffed with foam, handcuffed him to a chair where they painted his nails pink, then put on a pair of black tights, and a black cocktail dress. They did his make -up, mascara, lip gloss, foundation and eye shadow before one put a blonde wig on his head. Still not satisfied, they sprayed him with perfume, put on a necklace and finally a pair of three-inch stilettos. Only then did they set off around Dublin to get drunk.

Jason was set the task of not being noticed as a man for the whole weekend.

No-one noticed on Friday.

On Saturday, Chummy woke up tied to the bed, his makeup was freshly applied and he was dressed up again. That day he was wearing a black bra and panties with a white tank top, along with denim hot pants and knee high leather boots with a three-inch heel. That day they went paint-balling so he had to take extra shoes because he was trying not to be noticed. He spoke like a girl, walked like one, went to the toilet like one and carried a handbag.

At the paint-balling, between rounds, he did his make-up like the other girls, who were tagging along with the group of men, and who kept shooting at his bum.

That night they stayed in and played Drunken Twister. On Sunday, Chummy woke up once again tied up. Make up was applied and he was dressed again, although he didn't seem to be struggling so much now. That day he was wearing a different top, different black bra and panties, tight blue jeans and thigh-high leather boots. They were meant to be going karting but ended up going to the shopping mall instead, Jason still acting like a girl. He brought and tried on other clothes and make-up. After lunch they all went to watch him get a makeover and a manicure.

Chummy looked down at his nails, but Tom was

talking at him, expecting a reply.

'Brilliant stag do, Chummy. Brilliant! To think you went the whole weekend with no one noticing you were actually a man. Fancy that!'

'Yes, just fancy ...' said Chummy and sadly smiled.

Tentage   CMH

As he picked up his knife and fork to eat his breakfast, cooked to perfection by Betty, his adoring wife, Bert Oldcastle was elated.

'Eee lass', he said in his best Cockney accent. He liked people to think he'd been born within the sound of Bow Bells. He had, it was the pub across the road: he was a Glasgow Lancastrian. 'This is just how I like it. Charred bacon, eggs so runny they've still got see through whites, tommies that are still raw and burned in parts, cold beans and a cremated toast tombstone. Great!'

Having got properly started he continued around mouthfuls of food. 'The marquee hiring is going great guns. Every tent we've got's out on hire for the big match weekend. Except that ex-forces surplus one that I got when we was starting up that is. And,' he paused to remove some gravelled toast from under his upper denture, 'I had a call from the Trentby Golf Club last evening. They've got a last-minute booking and can't seat all two hundred guests inside. So that's going up for the first time in a few years as well. If I can get Jeff Smith and Freddy and Charlie and Dai together, we can have it up this afternoon. Provided that idle beggar Montgomery can get out of his equipment shed long enough to tell us were to put it, that is!'

Mrs Betty was concerned, her part in the business was to decorate the interiors. 'What's it for, Bert? I mean, if it's a wedding then we need different stuff to a party.'

'Dunno,' was the husbandly reply, 'didn't ask. Gareth didn't say and I didn't ask. Just do the best you can with what we've got left in the stock room. There's some of that floaty white stuff in there,' he continued, spraying toasted gravel and baked beans liberally over the table cloth, 'and a few flower stands and bits and bobs for tables. Just see what you can do, it'll be okay?'

Going into his office, as he grandly called the falling-apart shed at the back of his storage barn, Bert made a few phone calls and ticked 'Manpower' off on his list: Freddy, check, Charlie, Okay but he'll be late, and Dai, when he'd finished his postal round, according to Blodwen. Then on to the sticky one.

'Jeff? I've got a job for you today, lad ... yes, just for one day, but, next week it'll be at least four days work to take the lot down again ... I know you can earn more than I pay with your flop singing but you remember, I pay cash in hand, not cash sometime maybe from De Wrong! What's more you get free use of my truck to get all your rammel to those gigs, so think on! Enough Rudy ruddy Darkness and more Jeff Smith. Are you on or not?' He was.

It stood there in all its lack of glory. A dark green monstrosity that was showing signs of wear and tear, especially tear and definitely wear. It looked like a drop-out from some forces 'School of Camouflage', where it wasn't green, it was black or brown or off-white and where it wasn't any of those, it was in holes. Not big holes but, definitely, lacy looking. They'd stuck patches over the big ones; until they ran out of patches.

'It'll be all right as long as it doesn't rain too much, possibly,' was Jeff Smith's comment.

When Gareth, the club secretary, saw it, his comments turned the job into an education in the fine art of swearing, probably in several languages. Some of which may not have been human.

'Mrs Oldcastle,' he'd said, 'you've done a great job of turning this interior into a delight to the eye. Always providing that the eye in question is colour-blind in the visible spectrum.'

'I'm so glad you like it, Mr Gareth,' replied Betty. 'I didn't have a lot of time to work anything out, so I've done the best I can with what was available.'

'Such a riot of colour and so many different table decorations. I especially like those clever table leg covers. Very novel, Mrs Oldcastle. They completely hide the wonky legs, props and packing, mainly. But is there anything you can do about the lighting, do you think? I mean candles are all right as decoration, but not as main lighting. People like to see what they're eating.'

'I'll have a word with Bert about it. I'm sure that something can be done. Who's doing the catering for you, Mr Gareth?' quizzed Betty. 'I know your kitchens can't cope with two hundred covers.'

'No problem there, Mrs Oldcastle. I've got the help

of Luigi Stephano and his team. They'll be doing the main cooking at the College and finishing off here. No problem, he tells me.'

'What's on the menu, then? I like to keep up to date, you know!'

'We've agreed l'escargot to start, ragoût de lapin, with associated vegetables, of course, as a main course, and a traditional bread and butter pudding to follow.'

'That sounds ... interesting ... Mr Gareth. I wish you luck. But are you sure about the lighting? From what I've heard it may be a good idea if folks can't see what it is they've got on their plates!'

They wended their separate ways, Gareth still swearing under his breath.

Only a matter of time   JP

'Now, Mr Cross. I don't want you getting the idea this is some sort of exclusive. It's just that you're top of the list on the page in my phone book headed "Pains in the bleedin' backside". All the others'll get the same news later today.'

Well, thought Chris, a few hours advanced notice was the nearest thing to a thank-you the *Trentby Evening News* had come to expect from Inspector Bruce Wallace Mackay. 'News, Mr Mackay?'

'That's right. Shortly after 2pm yesterday two men were arrested in Liverpool. Derek and David Dodd of Trentby have been charged with a number of offences relating to the recent disappearance of taxis in the town. I am pleased to tell you that these arrests resulted from ...'

'... from the information passed on to the Police by *Trentby Evening News*,' interrupted Chris proudly.

'... from good, old-fashioned police work,' continued Mackay. 'We were alerted to the involvement of the Dodd brothers when one of our wooden-tops ... I mean, uniformed officers came across one of the missing taxis in Barbara Castle Mews as he pounded the beat.'

He pounded the beat alright, thought Chris, recalling that the officer in question had run into the taxi's boot on his bike as chased a couple of kids into Barbara Castle Mews and had left an impression of his rather large nose in the pavement.

'But I tipped you off where all the other taxis were,' objected Chris. 'When you said policing wasn't as easy as ABC it made me think the words "sea", "tea" and "hell" in the Isle of Man letter might stand for the letters "C", "T" and "L". Then I remembered when I flew to Ibiza for my holidays in the summer I parked my car in bay C9 at the airport. When I had a look, there were the taxis in bays marked C, T and L.'

'Just a loose end, Mr Cross. Just a loose end,' said Mackay dismissively. 'It was only a matter of time before I'd have got to the airport myself. Now, if you've got all that down, I'll bid you a good day.'

Chris Cross slammed the door on his way out and received a knowing smile from a passing constable as he muttered, 'One day, Mackay, one bleedin' day.'

FRIDAY

Spectacular   CMH

'Another six minutes if it's on time, Ace, but I would-
n't bet on it,' came from Doc Hollyweigh of Cavalry
Cabs as he leaned against Ace's cab outside the railway station.

Ace pulled a face as he replied, 'I've been consid-
ering getting another job. My mate in the haulage
business is looking for long-distance drivers.'

'You? Long-distance driving? Don't be daft, Ace!
Long hours, short breaks, away from home most
nights, it's a recipe for a broken home is that.'

'Well, all this hassle we're getting is ...', he was interrupted as his radio burst into life.

'Wingco to Kilo-Alpha-Hotel. Ace High, your pick-
up's been cancelled,' came Dusty's voice over the
radio. 'You're wanted at the Rover's footy ground
asap. Some footballer's poncy motor's been nicked
and he's thrown a benny about getting home. The
Plod don't reckon it's the Dodd brothers again. I
don't think so either 'cos you put 'em on the 11.25
train, didn't you?'

'Roger, Wingco,' Ace answered. 'Yes, the Dodd
boys got on it, bags and baggages. Over.'

'Bags and baggages? What's that supposed to
mean, Ace? Over.'

'Suitcases and girlfriends, Dusty. Off to sunny
climes they told me. Costawhatsit, I think they said.
Over and Out.'

As Ace pulled out Pat Walker reminded Doc over his radio, 'Get over to the opticians and get that eye-test certificate. Your appointment's in twenty minutes. Don't mess this one up!'

'Hmm,' had said the optician. 'Nothing much to worry about here, Mr Hollyweigh. Just a bit short-sighted in the left eye and long-sighted in the right eye. A pair of glasses will put that right. It'll take about ten days for them to arrive and then I'll be able to issue you with that certificate. Unless you want to wear contact lenses, of course? If you do, I may be able to give you a certificate this afternoon.'

Asking why the delay he was told, 'The specialist will be available then to show you how to put them in, remove them and take care of them. Once she's done that, I can re-test you and issue the certificate. But, as contact lenses can only be worn continuously for ten to twelve hours you'll need spectacles as well. However, you may be one of those people who can't wear contacts lenses. To check that, I'll put a pair in and you go off for a walk, or something, somewhere for three-quarters of an hour or so.'

After the forty-five minutes were up he returned to be told, 'Sorry, Mr Hollyweigh, you're allergic to the plastic. It's got to be spectacles and that's going to take seven to ten days. As you drive a taxi I'm required to report this to the local authorities, so I'd very strongly urge you to stay off the road until then.'

Olga's very popular! SMS

'He-llo, Lady Vee, your Goddess of the Morning. How

may I help you into paradise? Of course, Trentby Discreet Escort services welcomes new clients.

'Really?

'For the Mayor's daughter's wedding? Yes, we do have a selection of …. You know who you want … Righto … The Russian girl? You don't know her name …' Vera beamed into the cracked mirror she had hung up above her desk. 'The pretty one with the very long legs … I know just who you mean and you are in luck. Sasha is free,' she grimaced, crossing her fingers. Well, they couldn't all have Olga on their arm, could they?

'And your name is? Very well, Mr Cross, I'll send Sasha to meet you outside the front gate of the Church of the Bleeding Heart. You can't miss Sasha! I'll tell her to wear a pink carnation and you wear one too, dear. Now, if you could just read off that big number on your card.'

Gloria was ear-wigging; she had unwisely settled on her knees and was vainly attempting to follow the instructions supplied with the aforesaid chocolate fountain. Unfortunately, as these were printed in Japanese she was struggling with a series of pictures. 'You are a one, our Vera, he wanted Olga, didn't he?'

'This late notice, he'll be lucky to get anybody. The next punter gets saddled with Angie. That'll give them more than they bargained for.'

Gloria chuckled, 'She loves a good cry at a wedding.'

Vera shook her head at the mess of packets of screws scattered over the floor, 'Let's not dwell on Angie's waterworks, how the Dickens are we going to get this contraption put together? That looks like a warning notice to me.'

'Warning ... no, it's a guideline thingy, I think,' said Gloria, screwing up her bifocals and jabbing at the instruction sheet, her fingers sticky with melted chocolate. As Vera knelt to pick up a packet of leftover nuts and bolts the phone rang.

'He-llo, Lady Vee, your Goddess of the Morning. How may I help you into paradise? Of course, Trentby Discreet Escort Services always welcomes new clients.

'Really? For the Mayor's daughter's wedding? Yes, we do have a selection of ... You know who you want ...' a distinct feeling of déjà vu came over Vera as Gloria silently chuckled. 'The Russian girl ... I'll see what I can do ... Yes, we do have a Russian girl free on Saturday afternoon. I'll get her to meet you outside the church gate she'll be wearing a red carnation, so you wear one too, dear. And your name is? Righto Mr Bonnay, if you'll read off that nice big number on your card for me, dear.'

'Angie isn't Russian! She's from Bolton,' grinned Gloria and with a sharp tug managed to scatter the contents of a bag of washers all over the mat and under the chaise.

'That may be, but on Saturday she's from Moscow and she's escorting the Social Page Editor of the *Trentby Evening News*, a Mr Philip Bonnay, to the society wedding of the year.' Something about that name rang a bell but just at that moment Gloria performed a hat-trick with the screw packets sending six tiny screws from a packet with a big red number seven emblazoned on it rolling across the floor.

Cursing, Vera hitched up her skirt and knelt

down. Both women were heads down and bottoms up patting the floor in search of washers and screws as a voice in the doorway said, 'Eee, the sights you see!'

The vicar's dilemma   MH

William Warmer stood in front of the church and waited for Julian Hogg to arrive. He still could not understand why he had phoned the man in the first place. 'Okay, he was the only exorcist on the Web but Julian Hogg, for heaven's sake, the last person in the world I want to see,' he said and crossed himself as he realised what he had said.

He stood for a while and realised he could do with a drink to get him through meeting Julian again. He grabbed his hip flask and put it up to his mouth just as a huge limousine pulled up next to him.

'Still like a tipple, then,' said a happy voice from the open window.

'F-F-F-For m-m-m-medicinal purposes only,' William stuttered.

'Yeah right, you will keep believing that until your liver gives up the ghost,' he laughed.

But William didn't laugh.

'The ghost, get it?' Julian laughed even more.

'Very drôle, Julian. Very clever,' William sighed and looked at the man he had hated for so many years.

'Oh, come on, Willy. Where's your sense of humour?'

'Lost it about the same time I met you?'

'Oh, I see, this goes back to university days does it? Would it help if I apologised?'

'Not really. Let's forget and start afresh, shall

we?'

'Whatever you want! Now, lead me to this pesky poltergeist.'

Julian followed William into the church and immediately balloons full of water began flying through the air before hitting the floor and soaking both of them.

'Hey, William, I am practising for the wedding. Who's the geek with the glasses?' asked Trevor gleefully.

'Your worst enemy poltergeist,' shouted Julian.

'What do you mean my worst enemy?'

'You are not going to ruin the wedding because I am here to stop you,' Julian hissed.

'Yeah, right, fat man,' Trevor cackled.

'Believe it, poltergeist.'

'We will see about that,' said Trevor as he made two more water-filled balloons appear out of nowhere.

'Try throwing them, my translucent friend,' Julian smirked.

'Right, prepare to get wet.' Trevor tried to throw a balloon at the two of them but it went up into the air and landed on his head. 'What are you doing to me?' he wailed.

'Sending you back to where you belong. Now go you pesky, putrid poltergeist.'

'No, you can't do this. I must have my revenge on the famil ...' he shouted nervously as he saw his body disappearing. 'Please, William, stop him and let me stay. I promise I will be a good poltergeist.'

William kept quiet and watched Trevor disappear, leaving only the echo of his pleading echoing in the church.

'There you go, Willy, all done. Tell me where can I get a decent cup of coffee around here?'

'I'll put a pot on in the vestry. But, Julian, how did you manage to get rid of Trevor? I thought you had to chant or something.'

'The secret to this job is to keep them occupied while somebody else does the chanting. Hey, George, you can come out now,' he shouted and a figure with a crucifix appeared from behind the pews.

'Good thinking,' said William, relieved it was over. With a smile of satisfaction he showed Julian and his friend George to the vestry.

Flowers: Friday morning   EJW

Tarquine had completed the funeral flowers. 'Mom' and 'Dad' were the main tributes. Yuk, he hated named flower arrangements, so common. Apparently the two old dears were shopping when they were knocked over by a runaway trolley which had been pushed along by a toddler who had escaped from his mom. It may not have been fatal if the two dears had not collided with an eight-foot high stack of baked bean tins ... but when uncovered their long-life hessian bags were found to be covering their faces, cause of death asphyxiation. Their family had also decided an arrangement in the shape of a trolley was also a fitting tribute: Tarquine argued with this but they insisted; some people are so sensitive and thoughtful.

Sniffing came from the back of the shop, his work

-experience girl Martha Vinard, nicknamed 'Greensleeves' at school, was busy cutting the ends off red carnation stems.

'Oh, Martha, my love, how can you want to be a florist when you suffer with hay fever all year round?'

Martha looked at Tarquine through bloodshot eyes, 'I only had two choices, this and a trainee chef, didn't get through the first interview, couldn't understand why.'

Tarquine lifted his eyes to heaven, 'Never mind, sweetie, good job flowers always need watering.

'Martha, I have to leave soon to arrange the church flowers. That stupid mother of the bride has insisted on all red flowers, she originally wanted red and white. My godfathers! I said they should never be seen together, blood and bandages, Martha, blood and bandages. Eventually she agreed to just a mixture of reds, good job I have plenty of imagination — and greenery.'

'Oh, Tarquine, you are so clever and talented. I wish I could be like you,' she sniffed, wiping her red nose across her sleeve for the umpteenth time that morning.

Tarquine thought about his plans for tomorrow as he drove to the church. He had telephoned a taxi service called Cavalry Cabs. A lady called Pat Walker had confirmed the hire of a taxi to deliver both the funeral and wedding flowers to the stated addresses. She did say she only had one taxi to spare for the times he wanted but was sure the driver would be able to deliver both orders correctly as long as he labelled the arrangements. He chuckled to himself when he visualised what the outcome would be.

Tarquine pushed the church door with his elbow.

'Flaming churches,' he muttered. 'How can they make you feel welcome if it's so difficult to get in?'

'Hello, anyone here?' Tarquine called out, thinking better let them know I'm here. No reply. Silence.

He hauled the cardboard boxes into the aisle, then called, 'Hello,' whilst walking towards the vestry. The door opened, Tarquine squealed with delight;

'Oh, Tinkers! What are you doing here? I love your fancy dress costume, am I invited to the party?'

The Vicar adjusted his collar to relieve the blood rushing to his face, cleared his throat and began to give the hardest explanation of his life.

William, aka Tinkers, had tears in his eyes when he looked at Tarquine, 'I am so sorry. This is no fancy dress costume, this is the real me. Perhaps this is a good time for you to have found out my true identity.'

Tarquine gulped, snapping his gaping mouth shut, 'Crikey, it's certainly a surprise. I can't believe you're a man of the cloth. Does dressing up as a fairy make you feel nearer to the angels?' Tarquine felt his temper rising with the indignity of it all, 'I have really been taken for a fool this time. All my faith in humanity has flown out of the window together with you, Tinkers. Or should I call you William, the name shown on the parish notice board?'

William reached out to Tarquine, 'Yes, William is my real name. Please try to understand. I have been a stupid fool. Can I rely on your discretion and trust not to reveal our meetings or my little fetish? After all, you must know I'm not in love with you, I only used you as a fashion outlet and model for my dressing up. I am so sorry.'

Tarquine kept quiet, thinking to himself he needed time to sort this all out, then he smiled, 'I should have realised all was not right when you kept saying your prayers before waving your magic wand and scattering fairy dust all over me. Now, I have to arrange these wedding flowers before the rehearsal this afternoon, can we speak later? In the meantime I have one favour to ask, I need to be in hiding to watch the rehearsal. Can you arrange somewhere for me to hide?'

William smiled back at Tarquine giving a sigh of relief, perhaps everything was going to be all right after all, 'Of course, I will be happy to help with anything you need. See the red curtain at the back of the altar? You can hide behind there. Why do you need to do that anyway?'

Tarquine stared at him, his mind racing ahead trying to make plans but keeping Tinkers unaware of any future favours he may be asked to conform to.

'You asked for my discretion regarding our torrid situation, now I would ask you to ask no questions about what I need to do in the next twenty-four hours. No matter how strange the requests may be. I promise when this is over, I will disappear from your life for good.'

'Thank you, Tarquine, you have a kind heart. I'm sorry to have hurt you. You will need to be back here for half past two as the rehearsal starts at three.

Tarquine snapped back his reply, 'Fine, that's great. Now I really must get on with these flowers.

Can you leave me in peace to get on with my job?'

The church was cool and quiet when he returned later that afternoon, no sign of Tinkers or William the vicar, as he now thought of him. Tarquine slipped behind the curtain, preparing himself for the appearance of his one and only true-love, the bridegroom Chummy.

What would he do?

Would he be able to control himself?

Would revenge still be the one and only thing he wanted for getting back at Chummy?

The noise of the church door opening made Tarquine jump, he peeked through the curtain his heart thumping as he caught sight of Chummy. No change there then. He still loved him. The question now was, did Chummy still love him?

Cats out of bags   SMS

'He-llo, Lady Vee, your Goddess ... eh up, Bertha ... where's the fire? Oh, I see ... worry not, flower; leave it to Vera ... I'll get it sorted.' Vera cradled the handset as if it was made of eggshells.

'Trouble at mill?' spluttered Gloria, scratching her armpit with a darning needle. Gloria had a mouth full of ostrich feathers, vividly limp, in a violent shade of fuchsia, ostrich feathers, which she was attempting to stitch back on to Angie's moth-eaten feather boa ready for the approaching nuptials. Angie had used it in her stage act when, to the sound of the Dance of the Seven Veils, she would tastefully remove her garments and display her ample charms with an eight-feet python coiled round her nether regions. But ever since the unfortunate accident with the stage manager's puppy, Angie had kept the boa for sentimental reasons to remind her of Percy the python.

'That idiot Wingco has forgotten to pick Bertha up for the rehearsal and now he's got no cabs free for an hour, on account of two of his taxis being kidnapped this week.'

'Cab-napped,' tittered Gloria. 'It'll all be over by then,' she added, averting her gaze from Vera's frown.

'Nip down to the Copper Kettle, there's a luv,' smiled Vera pleadingly and showing off a top set of naked gums.

'Why me?' grumbled Gloria, stuffing saliva-soggy feathers back into the bag. 'Why can't you go to fetch the lazy beggars?'

'What if the phone rings?'

'Oh, all right. Does Ma'am have a preference or will any lazy beggar with a cab do?'

'Any. Just go and dig one out of the greasy spoon and get them back behind the wheel.' With no more ado, Vera ejected the still-protesting Gloria down the steps and waved her off in the direction of the cabby's favourite watering hole, the Copper Kettle Cafe on the corner of Market Street.

As Gloria's bottom waddled out of view, several seconds after her hat had disappeared round the corner, Vera had hardly had time to rescue her mug of tea from the microwave than the phone rang.

'He-llo, Lady Vee, your Goddess of the ... Oh, hello petal, I don't hear your dulcet tones in many a moon and then twice in ... what's the matter, Joanie? Stop crying, sweetie, I can't make out what you're saying. Deep breath! Good girl. You tell your Aunty Vera ... Goodness me, now that is serious. Are you sure? Lord FC? Flipping 'eck as like ... And you and Chummy err ... did, ... err, didn't you?

'Crikey! There's a name for that. My mother had a word for it! That's "in-a-vest", that is! When did your Ma let the cat out of the bag? Today! I see ... When she found out you were going to the wedding. This is definitely a two-cuppa problem to have a chin wag over. You have a walk over here. You'll never get a cab at this time of day, they've all being nicked, or they're parked up swilling tea. See you soon, sweetie, and if you see Gloria on the way. tell her to get her backside into gear. She'll be in the bookies, she always is when there's a crisis.'

Helium balloons   SMS

'He-llo, Lady Vee, your Goddess of the ... Oh, hello, Bertha, what's up? No ... really? Well, I go to the foot of our stairs ... I was just saying to Pat Walker ... Why was she here? She just popped in to check how many cars you needed for Saturday as we've changed the number required twice due to new escort bookings. Don't worry, your car is still booked. Anyway, I was just saying ... Oh, right,' Vera's mouth froze into a line as flat as a cut in best liver as her florid gossiping was curtailed by a list of instructions. She put down the receiver.

Carrying two mugs of tea around the jumble of half-completed wedding paraphernalia Gloria couldn't stop herself asking the obvious: 'Her ladyship in another bind, then?'

'Helium balloons? What the flaming heck are helium balloons? In pink neon with a photo of the bride and groom in a big love heart ... by Saturday. More than eight dozen. I mean, I'm good but am I that good, our Gloria? Young Britney's playing her face again, I expect. It wouldn't hurt her to do a hand's turn.'

'Wouldn't ordinary balloons do?' asked Gloria.

'She wants to let them off in a cloud as the happy couple leave for their honeymoon.'

'Better warn the airport then, could be a hazard to aircraft ... ' grinned Gloria, as the absurdity of a cloud of balloons wearing young Chummy's homely kisser being met at 30,000 feet by the pilot of a jumbo crossed her mind. 'Who's taking the photographs, by the way?'

Vera's jaw dropped open. The photographs. Who would be taking the pictures for the wedding album and the video now the wedding planners had gone bust? But, just at that moment the phone rang.

'He-llo, Lady Vee, your Goddess of the Morning. How may I help you into paradise? Oh, hello, Councillor Kelly, I was just wondering what had happened to you. You're a bit late calling for your appointment this morning. You naughty boy! Oh, I see ... well, have you found the key to the handcuffs? Down the back of the radiator? ... Jolly good. Now, have I mentioned the Special Offer? Oh dear, what a shame, in the book it says you've already exceeded your silver-star membership allowance, dear. You'll have a think about upgrading to gold-star service. There's an extra bonus visit from Miss Smith with her naughty chair, and 10% off any S&M costume hire for a limited period only.'

As Vera plonked 'Land of Hope and Glory' on the CD player for the titillation of the geriatric Chairman of the Industry and Enterprise Committee, better known for his empire-building in the area - there wasn't a street in the city centre that hadn't some frontage thrown up by Kelly Construction - rather than for his secret desires to be the favourite schoolboy for Sasha's 'Miss Smith' persona whose, 'You've been a very naughty boy!' sent him into heart-stopping shades of delirium.

Meanwhile, Gloria picked up the discarded Japanese instruction leaflet. Scratching the rigid perm in confusion, she gave the heap of components still to be inserted the once-over. She was sure the Leaning Tower of Pisa was straighter than the wonky waterfall they were building, and where did the melted chocolate go, and how did the pump thingy work, and why had the plug only got two wires?

Squinting sideways at the Heath Robinson contraption it was then that she remembered Pat Walker's cousin, Archie Cavendish: he'd have helium. After all, he had been building a Zeppelin in his shed on the allotments for donkey's years.

The photographer   SMS

'Is that you, our Melvyn? Oh, good lad, it's Aunty Vera. Bertha wants a favour. Bertha says nip round to Number 27 and pick up Angie's video camera ... Never mind that! She'll just have to pretend for the camera club. Half that lot wouldn't know which way up to hold a camera any way, they only go to the "cultural cinematic session" on a Thursday night to make fools of themselves drooling over Sasha taking her kit off.'

Gloria straightened up pushing her hands into the small of her lumbago as Vera hung up: 'Will he go, then?'

'Oh, yes, good lad is our Melvyn. He'll borrow his dad's taxi.'

'How is Wingco? Still umming and ahhing over Pat Walker's dulcet tones? He needs a good shove up his backside. Faint heart never won Fat Controller.'

'She's not fat. She's big-boned! Anyway, is that it? Is it finished?' said Vera, squinting and holding her head on one side as she tried to work out which way up the chocolate fountain was supposed to stand on the plinth.

'Best I can do,' smiled Gloria, scratching a stray verucca with a knitting needle.

'And, only three bolts and a couple of washers left over. Not bad, our kid! Not bad.'

Before Gloria could own up to the handful of other mechanical thingies she was holding on to behind her back, the phone rang.

'He-llo, Lady Vee, your Goddess of the Afternoon. How may I help you into paradise? Oh it's you Mr Philpott. What a nice surprise. It'll save me a call. I must come and see you about my top set, wobbling all over the place, so it is. Very distracting for my

127

clients when I can't get my f's and s's sorted out, you know. Professional diction is very important in my area of expertise. Talking of which, is it the "drilling-and-filling" special as usual? The price has gone up, I'm afraid, but the good news is we've a special on this week: BOGOF. Give me a minute to put my top set back in and away we go … there we are … I knew I'd got it somewhere. Lovely voice that fellah, one of my favourites. Shall I sing along? A one, two, three, four … I'm a red toothbrush, you're a green toothbrush … What's the matter, dear, isn't that right?'

Shaking her head Gloria binned the offending packet of left-over bits as she made for the loo: she hated dentists. Vera was on her own this time. Besides, more importantly, who did she know who could take photographs besides Melvyn?

Melvyn lived for the camera club and he'd do anything for Angie. What a sweetheart that boy was! Pity about his affliction, but what's an odd twitch or two amongst friends? And besides, the bouts of flamboyant expletives reacted well to sticky toffee and the calming influence of her hand in his pocket, according to Angie, and she should know.

Gloria grinned, the young rascal had been sharing cornflakes with Aunty Angie three mornings a week for quite a while, unbeknownst to Bertha.

That was another secret she wouldn't be sharing with Cousin Vera.

Archie and Melvyn's confusion   SMS

'He-llo, Lady Vee, your Goddess of the … oh, hello, Archie … you got the message, then? Speak up, lad, what's that noise in the background? A chain saw, yes, of course it is … I should have guessed. Now, have y'got any helium Bertha can borrow for these balloons?'

Gloria's eyes rolled towards the heavens. Vera's grasp on things of a scientific nature was indeed suspect. Even she knew borrowing things of a gaseous nature didn't seem right somehow.

'You have! Oh, good lad! I'll send Melvyn round this afternoon. You won't be there? Oh. Righto, that's a good idea.' The call ended abruptly as Vera swung round to watch Gloria who was packing the wobbly chocolate fountain into two black bin bags marked 'Garden Refuse Only' ready for the short journey to the golf club.

'Sorted?' asked Gloria, with a voice full of more hope than expectation.

'Sorted. He'll leave the shed door open. Melvyn can go in and help himself to a canister.'

Gloria's face darkened, but before she could voice concerns of impending doom, the phone rang.

'He-llo, Lady Vee, your Goddess of the Morning. How may I help you into paradise? Eee, hey up, our Bertha, I was just about to ring you. I've sorted out the helium for the balloons, and Gloria's taking the fountain to the golf club any minute now. Ace is taking her.'

Gloria nodded in affirmation as Ace's cab pulled

onto the forecourt. With a wave she trundled down the portacabin steps and beckoned to Ace with a bent finger. Ace didn't like finger-beckoning, it reminded him of dog training with Barbara Whatshername. Ace didn't like dogs.

'There's no need for me to go, is there, cherub? Just drop this off lot off at reception, there's a luv.' With that Gloria palmed the tenner given to her by Vera for the two way trip and passed Ace a fiver.

'Good man, knew I could rely on you. Drop me off at the bookies. It's on the way.'

Vera watched Gloria driving away in the cab and crossed off one item on her 'To Do' list. 'Brilliant – fountain and helium.' Before Vera could concentrate further on Bertha's list of instructions, the telephone rang and Vera was once again called upon to assist one of her elderly flock into sticky oblivion: Aubrey Gascoigne, head waiter at the Crown Hotel for thirty years. He and Bertha had had an understanding for nearly as long.

'Bolero, sweetheart?' asked Vera, putting her teeth in and digging out her best rounded vowels, 'I've slapped on a ten per cent discount as usual.' Aubrey was almost family, which, if she'd had time to consider, was deeply disturbing on several levels.

At that moment Gloria, clutching a windfall-fiver destined for the nose of the favourite to win the 3.30 at Epsom, was showing too much pink bloomer as she struggled out of the cab outside the bookies in Bridge Street. Ace gave an enormous backside a friendly shove to assist his passenger onto the pavement and shot off into the traffic.

The reception, she said. She must mean the Mayor's Do. He'd check with Wingco.

'Kilo-Alpha-Hotel to Control. Come in, Wingco. Over.'

'Control to Kilo-Alpha-Hotel. What's the problem, Ace?'

'Saturday Wedding? Where's the reception at again? Over.'

'Golf Club, Ace. Get a move on, a fare's waiting in Duke Street. Over and out.'

Balloons   SMS/CMH

'Hello, Vera. I've got the balloons you ordered. I was going to make a special trip to the wholesalers, as it was more than I had in stock, and as it was short notice. But, I've managed to do a special deal for you. Sort of second-hand, never been used, with a smart logo on the back. Should be all right 'cos they'll only blow away anyhow. I'll have the printing done by closing time, so can you get somebody to collect them?' The harassed joke shop man, whose own sense of humour had been abraded away over the years of selling jokes, pondered the order as he put the phone down on the answer machine.

'Three hundred balloons with that ugly mug plastered all over them,' he yelled sometime later, to his assistant over the sound of the printing machine, 'What's the world coming to? Still we don't have to fill them, that's a relief. Where's she going to get the gas from? Helium tanks don't grow on trees you know, and it'll take flaming ages to fill that many. Oh, well, not our worry.'

'Phew,' said Vera to Gloria, as she put the phone down, 'that's that! Three hundred balloons ready for collection in the morning. We'll have them blown up in no time with that gas from our Archie. I'll get Wyatt to pick them up.'

Keeping her own counsel Gloria wasn't so sure. Three hundred seemed a lot more than eight dozen.

SATURDAY

Early morning   YL

'Von, the cake's here.'

Janice's excited daughter ran into the kitchen, but came to an abrupt halt. 'Mummy, shouldn't there be three boxes?'

'The bloke only left this one. You'd better check it.'

'Yvonne opened the box gently. Maybe, she thought, he'll bring the others up in a minute. As it was opened Janice gave an audible gasp and her daughter started to scream uncontrollably.

Jim Jones, hearing the commotion rushed into the kitchen. 'What the hell?' He was just in time to see his daughter faint to the floor. Jim was about to pick her up when he, too, noticed the cake. He stepped over his daughter, 'Give me the baker's number,' he demanded, 'and see to your flaming daughter.'

'Yes, this is Councillor Jim Jones, we've had the wrong cake delivered,' he boomed down the phone. 'Which one's this? It appears to be two men in bed, in bondage gear, with "Happy Birthday, Sweetnuts" plastered all over it!'

Jim, who was by now a puce colour, shouted, 'What?'

Yvonne, now awake, said, 'Where's my cake, Daddy?'

'On its way to chuffing Glasgow, where else would it be?'

Jim told the woman on the other end of the phone to sort it out, before slamming the receiver down.

Yvonne hearing this, started to scream again. 'Shut up will you, for heaven's sake?' Jim picked up the carving knife and was about to shred the offending cake to pieces when they heard a loud banging on the front door. Before any of them could make a move, the front door was smashed off its hinges.

'Police!' they heard from the hall.

Typically, Yvonne chose this moment to faint again into her father's arms.

'Put the knife down, sir,' the police officer calmly warned Jim.

'But officer, I was only ...'

'I won't warn you again,' the officer told him.

'You've got this all wrong ...'

Janice watched horrified as mace was sprayed into her husband's eyes.

''Cuff him,' was the last thing she heard before, totally bewildered, she too hit the floor.

Still more balloons   CMH/SMS

The previous morning saw Vera and Gloria busy in-
flating the balloons from the wrongly collected
'hydrogen' tanks, and being from Archie, there was
no warning label saying this isn't helium. A big red-
painted letter 'H' could have meant anything.

A quick knot and release and each floated to the
ceiling to be trapped there until an errant draft
moved them away. A few got too near the light fitting
and popped, but they were ignored in the general
panic.

'Hello, Aunt Vera,' came Wyatt's voice from the
doorway, just before five-o'clock. 'What's this about
balloons for the golf club, then?'

'Shut that damned door, the blighters are escaping,'
snarled Gloria as a dozen balloons made an   escape
bid over Wyatt's head. Wyatt hadn't been a faux cowboy for nothing – he'd been paid – so he quickly batted most of them 'stray dawgies' back into the corral
of the portacabin.

'Humm! You need a net for these,' he said. 'Got
any bin bags they'll do at a pinch?' Fifty bin bags
later he was grimly hanging on as he tried to fit as
many as he could into his car through the window.

'Right, that's the cab full! Now let's see how many
we can get in the boot.'

It took three trips before he could take the old
girls, as he called them, home. 'Okay, girls, you got
everything? Handbags, glasses, the lot? Everything
off, taps turned off, lights out, the lot?'

He received a: 'Yes! Let's go, I'm fed up with these

balloons,' from Gloria as she went down the steps to get in the taxi.

Vera said, 'Just a minute. I've got to put the burglar lights timer on,' and plugged a rather tatty timer into the kettle socket as she passed. 'There, that's it until tomorrow.'

Before the wedding   EJW

Tarquine locked the flower shop. Hoisting his suitcase into his car, he headed towards the church; he needed to be in hiding before anyone else arrived. Once there he hid behind the curtain as before. The flowers had already arrived and had been placed on the steps leading to the altar. What joy, the trolley arrangement faced 'Mom' and 'Dad', both being surrounded by a number of colourful wreaths of various shapes and sizes, making the church look like a pantomime scene instead of a wedding.

William suddenly appeared from the vestry and gasped with a look of horror on his face. Tarquine covered his mouth with his hand to stifle a giggle, which was trying very hard to escape.

William walked towards the church door, his hands covering his face. He hoped the dreadful flowers would disappear. How was he going to get through the service or, the rest of the day; in fact the rest of his life. He'd be the laughing stock of the whole parish but, what could he do? He must keep his promise to Tarquine or his fairy days would be over. No magic wand was going to make this lot disappear. He stood outside the front door waiting to welcome the wedding party and guests, his vestments clinging to his sweaty body.

Weird or what? Chummy arrived with Tom, his best man, and the ushers in an old charabanc. The morning at home had been horrendous: the wedding flowers hadn't been delivered to the Jones's flat; telephone calls between the families grew as fast and hot as a comet's tail. Something about an S&M cake was lost in translation, Mrs J was screaming and crying at his stepmother while Yvonne had fainted at the news of funeral sheaths with cards of condolence tied to them. Frantic calls to the florist were answered by a recorded message advising the shop was shut for refurbishment.

Cavalry Cabs were contacted and blamed for the obvious mix-up, but the driver could not be contacted. He had done the delivery and gone to the football match. Tom was dispatched to church with a box of ivy, rapidly cut from the garden, together with a reel of cotton, and ordered to tie bunches of said ivy into buttonholes for the men. He sat in the church porch industriously cutting and wrapping cotton round the ivy like a gypsy getting ready to sell his wares.

Chummy breathed a sigh of relief when Tom's task was eventually completed and he pulled his buttonhole through his lapel and headed down the aisle. He stopped halfway, turning to Tom and said, 'At least the church looks cheerful. Those flowers make it look a bit like a stage production, but then that's what weddings are.

'Both Moms and Dads will love that one made just

for them and the trolley will give a hint to Yvonne of things to come. Not sure what the crosses and rings mean, but all in all whoever thought of it did a great job.'

Tarquine chuckled to himself and whispered, 'That's my boy. Chummy always was easy to please. I should have known he would be too naïve to spot someone was trying to sabotage his wedding. I'll leave him in peace and sweet innocence of my involvement. Time for this queen to abdicate and disappear into a new life in far away fairyland.'

Paperwork   CMH

Philip Bonnay was astounded. He'd never seen so much traffic packed into the twisting, medieval streets of Trentby.

By Order of the Mayor, the road works had been shut down for the big match weekend, and the police did their best to keep things moving. Of course, thought Philip, Yvonne, his daughter, is getting married today so that must have been a boost in that direction.

Still, he told himself, I'll be going there, as part of the press coverage admittedly, but with Olga on my arm. That means we'll get good seats at the reception. Got to be good has that!

'Phil, we need lots of pictures of that wedding you're covering. I'll take the cine-camera along to the match; you get stills with the new Nikon.' The barked instructions came across the office from Chris Cross, the Chief Reporter at the *Trentby Evening News*. 'Nip along to the golf club and get some preliminary stuff, menu, flowers and the like. We need to get in with the staff there. If there's time, you can get some stuff from the Bleeding Heart and have a few words from the Vicar as well.'

Philip, who knew that Cross had applied for one of the few membership places available at the golf club, thought: You mean you need to get in with the pro at the club.

'In this traffic it'll be quicker to walk to the church than try and drive, it's only about half a mile. I don't know about the golf club. Anyway, that's in the other direction, so it'll be quicker to come back here first.' He walked out singing, 'Get Me to the Church on Time'.

After silently shuddering at the tentage and lack of parking arrangements at the club and, after agreeing with Gareth that it was as good as could be expected in the circumstances, he returned, very slowly, to the office.

The footpaths were as crowded as the roads when the church came into view. The police had placed crush barriers in readiness around the front and had a man on the door.

'Morning, Josh! How's Margi today?' asked Philip, who lived across the street from him.

'Morning, Phil,' he replied. 'Much better, thanks. Just something she ate, we think. You know what kids are like, up one minute and down the next. You covering the wedding, are you?'

'That's me. Specialist in weddings, funerals, political party punch-ups, accidents, court reporter and general purpose dogsbody,' he answered. 'Can I go in and get some pictures? I need to interview the vicar and get some prelim stuff.'

'You're lucky there, Phil. Mr Warmer stuck his nose out about five minutes ago. Try the vestry; down the bottom on the left.'

'Will do. Thanks, Josh.'

As the reporter entered the normally gloomy, somewhat tawdry interior, he noticed that it sparkled. Light was glinting off highly-polished brass and wood-work, the altar was glowing in gold and scarlet, and the floor shone like glass. Flowers in great mounds and wreathes stood in alcoves and niches, and at the ends of the pews. This was going to be a wedding and a half.

He took the incoherent and muffled answer to his knock as permission to enter, only to find the vicar in his long johns holding an oversized fairy costume in his hand.

'What do you think?' he asked, 'Will it fit, do you think?'

Phil couldn't help it. He assumed a critical air, teased out the material, noted a maker's label at the back, and pulled an acidic face.

'Hmm! Not really, well made, you know. Not cut on the cross, as it were. Some of this stitching's a disgrace, skimped on the seams. It'll probably be all right for a fancy dress ball. But, if you party too energetically, and those seams go, it won't even cover your confusion. Wear it a bit and see. If it feels all right after an hour, it'll probably be okay to use but watch those gussets. They're the weak point.'

'You think so?' said William.

'Pretty sure,' Philip answered. 'My sister went to a party in something like that once. Only stood the one wearing.' He carefully didn't say that she tore it off in a six-year-old's temper tantrum.

Just before the wedding   SMS

'Eee, hey up, look at me ... I'm filling up ...' spluttered Vera, wetly dabbing her eyes with the tea towel. 'Always the same at weddings. Can't contain the pent up emotions buried deep within.'

'Don't be so wet, you daft ha'ppeth. Don't you get my frock soggy, it's hired from Madam Mordebt's. Here give me a hand with this hatpin,' said Bertha in her 'I'm in charge voice'. Bertha's head-creation was only the size of the Albert Hall and similar in colouring, a lacy concoction of brick-red with butter-cream piping that contrasted with the salmon-pink satin, mother of the bride type outfit she had also hired for the occasion.

'Very tasteful,' chipped in Gloria, wafting fag smoke out of the open door. 'And love those shoes ... can't wear stilettos me ... and hopeless with toe-post diamante ever since I had me bunions done.'

'Spare us dear ... spare us,' said Bertha, dismissing Gloria's foot fetish and casting an approving eye over Olga, who had, that very second, appeared from the Ladies. Olga glowed vitality in a tightly fitting, dove-grey suit trimmed with lace of dark smoky grey that matched a pillbox hat with a face veil, which allowed tantalising glimpses of her eyes.

'Oh, look at you … straight out of Madam Mordebt's window display,' cooed Vera, fingering the sleeve of the jacket in envy. She was right. Olga looked stunning. Bertha took that one on the chin and carried on regardless; gone was the day when she could have knocked the Olgas of this world into a cocked hat, but she was wise enough to rise above the cruelty of time and move on.

'Are we late?' chimed Angie and Sasha as they waddled into the portacabin, fluttering false eyelashes, and with feathers awry. 'We've had to walk: couldn't get a cab anywhere. And me in these shoes.'

'The ugly sisters have arrived,' whispered Gloria unkindly. Vera's nose grew pointy round the nostrils, but she forgave the remark; after all, Gloria was still smarting that her own invitation must have been lost in the post.

'Here you are, girls; here's your carnations. Now, when you get to the front of the church, the punter will find you by the colour of your flowers. Simple. Any fool can manage that!'

With that, Vera passed round the flowers and helped pin them on, which was a bit of a challenge for Angie and Sasha. They had both plumped for ruffled low necks and strappy straps which in Vera's professional opinion, was a bit tarty for the occasion … but then again, as Bertha said, they were being very well paid to go to this event. It was a professional escort engagement, not a jolly.

Smiles painted on, the four women descended

the steps. All went well until, attempting a hearty wave of farewell, Angie's fulsome balcony bra over-balanced her on the top step and all four went base over apex, landing softly on the mother of the step-mother of the groom's Albert Hall chapeau.

Olga's just learned some more useful Anglo-Saxon vocabulary, thought Vera, trying not to grin.

Previously . . . the groom sets off   CMH

At The Mansions it was controlled chaos.

Cousin W3 was keeping well away from that part of the house because they all seemed to have gone crazy. But there again, he now thought all his English relatives were crazy! Pretty nice on the whole; but still crazy.

Jason, walking about in a pair of boxer shorts, was wondering if he should get married at all, much less to Yvonne. Tom had a hangover and was throwing up in the en suite – some best man he had turned out to be.

'Britney, where did you put the studs to my dress-shirt?' shouted Sir Lancelot, pacing in his socks and gaiters, 'And get some clothes on, woman! Wandering about stark naked won't find them and it'll upset the staff.'

'I'm looking for my shoes, Lance. You know; those glitzy ones with the four inch heels. I'm sure they were in the dressing-room cupboard. Here they are! In your side, and I've got the studs as well. You see, I knew I'd put them somewhere safe!'

As she found Lancelot's studs, inside her shoes, Britney stuck a be-rollered head out of the door and shouted down the hall. 'Do get a move on, Jason! The taxis are due in twenty five minutes and you've not started dressing yet.'

The extremely temporary staff, now more extremely temporary than ever, were trying not to notice the chaos, and huddled in the kitchen.

Half an hour later all five of the groom's party were standing in the hallway waiting for the taxis to roll up, with Tom looking greener than ever, clutching a basket of ivy as so instructed.

'I'll just phone and see what's happening, Lance. It's probably a traffic jam, or something, but let's be sure.' Britney was getting concerned; if they had to walk all that way she was going to say something very impolite.

The phone in the Cavalry Cabs office was answered by Pat who assured Lady Britney that the taxis, as instructed by her Ladyship, had blue ribbons fitted and were on the way to Clement Attlee Towers to pick up the bridal party.

'There could be a delay as the traffic's the worst I've ever known,' Pat told Britney. What she didn't say was that there was, owing to them being impounded for evidence-collection, also a shortage of taxis.

'No! No! I ordered them for here at the Mansions,' Britney yelled. 'Never mind the Mayor's party. Where's *my* cab! I have to be there first, you know not the bride. She can wait.'

Working on the idea that 'The customer is always

right', Pat, who had known Lady B ever since she was a runny-nosed nipper hanging round the knocking shop, said, 'Hang on to your draws, petal. I'll do what I can,' and, with that, geed up the radio.

'Can't do, Pat.' Billy the Kid was stuck in a mega traffic jam in the Council House one-way system and moaned, 'I haven't turned a wheel for ten minutes.' Hoppy had also broken down; again! Wyatt was livid, 'Charging the battery, Pat. I'll be ages.' Having had his cab nicked and impounded as evidence, he was reduced to driving the spare cab, which wasn't up to much, and was still in the yard.

Doc was next on her list. 'Sorry, sweetheart. Flight's late.' Doc was on an airport run, waiting in the car park. Eventually Wyatt had stuffed Bertha, Angie and the others into his cab as they'd reached the corner of Bridge Street and was on the way to the church but was also delayed in slow-moving traffic. Not a lot of hope there, then, for Lady B. When she phoned Dusty she was told, 'Nightmare, Pat, right balls-up!' which she interpreted to mean that much the same situation applied at Concorde.

When she asked, Dusty said, 'Well, sweetheart, Biggles and Momma Classidy are up at the Clem Attlee trying to sort out who's going with whom and when. Momma says the Mayor's in a right old strop, he's been arrested about some cake-misunderstanding. Ginger's alongside Billy in that traffic jam, and Ace can't get across the river 'cos some flaming lorry driver's been and gone and got stuck.'

As the minutes ticked by, Jason, now proud part-owner of Trentby Weddings & Limousine Hire Co Ltd, had an idea. 'I'll get one of my drivers to pick us up,' he announced to the startled group.

'What drivers?' growled his father. 'Talk sense, you haven't got any drivers!'

'Oh, sorry, didn't I tell you? W3 and I are the new owners of Trentby Weddings. All I've got to do is get one of my drivers here and it's all solved.'

'I'll believe it when I see it!' grumbled his disbelieving parent. 'You couldn't run a ...' suddenly changing his mind about what he was saying.

Jason picked up the phone and spoke to the booking clerk-cum-driver-cum-everything else, who was left from the staff of the defunct Trentby Weddings.

'Righto, pater! A limited service is all that's available at such short notice. I don't know which vehicle it will be, but Archie Cavendish says he will be here in ten minutes.'

True as his word ten minutes later a rickety old bus negotiated the drive and stopped outside the Palladian entrance in a cloud of blue smoke.

Wiping his hands on an oily rag, 'Nice day for it,' grinned Archie, who had found his top set for the occasion. Pity about the greasy boiler suit, but you can't have everything.

'You have got to be joking! I'm not getting into that thing.' Sir Lancelot was obviously not au fait with the latest ideas on wedding transportation.

Britney, deciding that Women's Lib had better take a hand, seized her husband by the arm and propelled him into the charabanc. As soon as they were all aboard Archie started humming 'Get Me, to the

Church on Time' under his breath and, with a lurch and clank of gears, the groom, biting his nails, finally set off for his wedding.

Showdown at Clement Attlee Towers JP

It was always the same. Whenever Biggles decked out his taxi for a wedding, thoughts of his own nuptials came flooding back - just as if it were yesterday ... and look what a pigging awful day yesterday was, he smiled ruefully. Neither he nor his wife were more than kids when they tied the knot and, true to form, inside two years she'd run off with his best mate. How I've missed him, mused Biggles.

Today wasn't exactly the same as usual, though. 'The Wedding of the Year' was how the *Evening News* described it in a four-page supplement sponsored by Trentby International Chippy, the preferred eatery of the bride and her family. And today, as Biggles and Momma Classidy headed for Clement Attlee Towers to pick up the bridal party, their cabs were decorated in red, not white. This was, Dusty had assured him, on account of the family's Labour affiliations and in no way reflected on the bride's reputation, although Biggles half-remembered hearing in the pub ...

'Control to Kilo-Bravo-Oscar. Come in, Kilo-Bravo-Oscar.'

'Kilo-Bravo-Oscar to Control. Come in, Wingco,' replied Biggles, adjusting the volume on his radio.

'What's your ETA? Over.'

'Should be at the Towers in five minutes, Dusty.'

'Top hole, Biggles. By the time you've poured the

bride's mother and her hair-do into your cab and Momma's loaded up the bridesmaids, Ginger should be there for the bride and His Worshipfulness. The others'll mop up the rest. Over.'

'Wilco, Wingco. Over and out,' Biggles turned his wipers up a notch as the rain got heavier. Good job there's a canopy-thing over the front door of the Towers, he thought. He could do without them moaning about their windswept hair and runny make-up all the way to the church ... and the women are just as bad, chuckled Biggles.

'What the blood and stomach pills ...?' As Biggles turned into the car park at Clement Attlee Towers, His Worshipfulness the Mayor was in full rant at Wyatt Twerp, whose Cavalry Cab was parked under the far end of the entrance canopy with blue ribbons billowing across the bonnet.

'A booking? A booking? I don't give a f-f-floating voter if you were told you had a booking. Who in their right mind would expect me Leader of the Trentby Labour Party, to set foot in a car with BLUE ribbons?' bellowed Jim Jones, his face as crimson as his wedding cravat.

'By tradition every bride has to have "something borrowed, something blue", Mr Mayor,' smiled Wyatt, trying desperately to defuse the situation.

'Something blue? Well, if she has, sunshine, it had better be something frilly and out of public view. Now, get out of the way and let the car my wife *did* book take us to the bleeding church.' He waved at Biggles to drive under the canopy, behind Wyatt, 'I'll tell the Lady Mayoress you're here.'

Biggles reversed under the canopy behind Wyatt's car so as to leave himself a clear getaway and signalled to Momma to back up in front of him. He got out of his car for a word with her when the sound of screeching tyres filled the air. 'It's Ginger,' shouted Momma above the din, 'and that looks like that twonk Hopalong from Cavalry Cabs trying to get in front of him.'

Both cars headed towards the entrance but at the last minute, Ginger threw his cab into a handbrake turn and came to rest in front of Momma's car, his rear doors just in the shelter of the canopy, so Hopalong drove on round the back of the Towers to rendezvous with Wyatt who was on the radio.

Right on cue, the Lady Mayoress led the bridal party through the front door and, after much pushing and shoving accompanied by squeals from the bridesmaids and more bluster from the Mayor, the principals were loaded into the three cars. As Ginger moved off, Wyatt Twerp yelled out, 'We *did* have the booking!' Hopalong threw his cab into gear, drove around the car park and headed at speed for the oncoming Ginger.

When the noise of the impact subsided, Biggles opened his eyes. Ginger's cab was parked on top of the Cavalry Cab but the screams and shouts from both cars suggested everyone had survived the ordeal. Then, slowly, Hopalong opened his door, climbed onto the roof of the car and pulled Ginger through the window. They hit the ground in a heap and set about knocking seven bells out of each other. Not even the Mayor could deter them as he leant out of the car and demanded to be got down in language that, as far as Biggles was aware, didn't usually feature in the wedding ceremony.

Momma and Biggles decided it was time to leave, and Ginger extricated himself from Hopalong's bear-hug just in time to see Momma clip the front of his wing as she headed for the car park exit. The car slid to the ground and Ginger leapt in the driver's seat. As Biggles saw through his mirror that the bridal party formation was all present and correct, Ace and two other Concorde Cabs, arriving to pick up the rest of the guests, flashed their lights in unison. With a sigh of relief, Biggles glanced in his mirror at the Lady Mayoress. 'You alright back there?' he asked.

'Alright?' gasped the Mayoress, 'I'll never be alright again. No mother expects to see her daughter perched on top of a screaming cabbie.'

Biggles smiled as he remembered what it was that he'd heard in the pub.

Get me to the church CMH

"ello, 'ello, 'ello. Now then, what's a-goin' on 'ere, then?' Those immortal words could only be used by the long arm of the law, embodied in this case by Trentby's only pavement storm trooper, Traffic Warden Joe Cavendish (Archie's brother). 'Are you in charge of this lorry 'ere? This lorry what's illegally parked and ah-blockin' the pavement thereby ah-stoppin' folks ah-goin' about their lawful h-occasions? Also ah-stoppin' the Mayor and others gettin' in like we been told to keep an eye open special for.'

The small lorry emblazoned 'Grants Funeral Directors & Monumental Masons' was parked on double-yellows across the lych-gate of the Church of the Bleeding Heart. The masons were busy wrestling an unwieldy chunk of recently-mended, Gothically-ornamented stonework destined to re-adorn a mausoleum – belonging to the Fortesque-Chumleigh's - onto a totally inadequate trolley. Much colourful language was used to oil the movement, until the trolley was pushed into the gateway, where it met the first serious obstacle on its journey.

A porcine, overdressed woman wearing a hat the size and colour of the Albert Hall and a pair of earrings that classified as weapons of mass destruction approached. Her back-up team of an Anglo-Saxon shieldmaiden, a plump lady all-in wrestler and a decidedly dishy duchess-type were all armed with six-inch stiletto heels. The masons knew when they were out-gunned, and tried to get the trolley out of the way.

Unfortunately, Murphy's Law was working time-and-a-half and was saying, 'You may have got it in that way, but there's no way you're going to get it out!'

'Flaming hell, what idiot arranged for that monstrosity to be delivered today?' Bertha asked of no-one in particular. Then, recognising one of the delivery men, asked, 'Ernie Peacock, what the Dickens are you doing delivering this today, of all days? Get it shifted!'

'Oh, hello, Bertha,' came the softly-voiced reply, as if he didn't want to be seen talking to her; he didn't. 'Had a breakdown yesterday and thought we could

Bertha, Angie and Sasha all dressed up with somewhere to go

slip in and out quick today. Should have been alright but, what with the traffic and everything, we got held up. Hang on a couple of ticks while we get it shifted.'

Bertha gave a disbelieving 'Humph!' in return and stood back to get a quick fag in while she was waiting.

As the men hauled on the tow-bar to move the trolley, there came a screeching, grinding, sound from under the load; the back wheels sagged into a tired, inward-leaning, position. The masonry ensured that it was not going to be moved by leaning on the inside of the gate, and a precariously perched half-bag of quick-setting cement fell onto the floor, spilled, and dried up the puddle readily placed to receive it.

For a few seconds there was complete silence as they all took in the scene, then all hell descended on the hapless Ernie Peacock. Or at least Bertha, togged up in her best hired going-to-a-wedding kit, did.

She screeched, 'And just how are we to get to the church for the wedding, may I ask, Ernie Peacock?' It wasn't so much a question as a declaration of war. She continued, 'The bride and groom will be along shortly, not to mention Sir Lancelot and Lady Britney, the Mayor and Mayoress, most of the councillors, and just about all of the nobs around here. How are we all to get in now?'

'Well, you could always use the other gate,' the hapless man offered.

'What other gate? You blithering idiot,' came out at full volume, 'that means going all the way round and through the shopping centre!'

'Excuse me, pleaze,' came the dulcet tones of

Olga. 'Perhabs ve could climb owfer de vall ver it 'ave vallen. Or ver is de … de … *old* steps?'

Squeezing past the statue was impossible and climbing the wall out of the question; which left the 'Old Steps' and a less than perfect pathway half-hidden behind a yew hedge. Determined to get a good seat, Bertha tackled the challenge head on.

Although uneven and overgrown the steps were passable. It was the well-rusted iron gate that presented a serious obstacle. Bertha gave it a shove, but this gate had a serious attitude problem. Bertha backed up to get a run; and charged full bore. Bouncing from the metal work hurt her pride more than anything it did to her clothes, especially when Olga calmly walked to the gate and easily pulled it open a few inches to lithely eel her way through and regain the main path.

Sasha turned to Angie, gave a pitying look and said, 'We'll never get through that … I'm going through the shopping centre, Angie. It's only about four hundred yards and that won't spoil my glad-rags. You coming?'

As they left, Bertha waged war on the unfortunate Ernie by giving the statue a hard shove. This moved it just enough to slide down and smash onto the ground; leaving room for her to squeeze triumphantly past saying, 'I can't see Jim Jones being a happy bunny; climbing over this fallen angel when he arrives with the bride, Ernie. Can you?'

Vanity . . . Vanity . . . All is vanity . . .

Kilt awry Inspector Bruce Wallace Mackay sprinted across the churchyard after his escaping hair piece.

At the church door   SMS

'Ohh, you both look zo lovely,' oozed Olga, shivering as eventually the three girls huddled together in the doorway of the Church of the Bleeding Heart, ignoring the sniffs and frowns of righteous married ladies of the town who were pushing their way inside. A number of their husbands had acquired a crick in their necks and were examining the red carpet pathway as they scurried passed the gaudy trio praying for a lack of recognition.

At that moment, as Trentby City's unmarked CID car drew up on double-yellows, Bertha, who had been massaging her bunions by the lych-gate, hurriedly approached the girls on tottering heels waving her gloved hand to all and sundry who were wearing trousers, in a general gesture of bonhomie to her extensive over-50s client-list.

'He's here, sweetie, big smile, flash those ivories.'

As one the three girls did their best to say 'cheese'. Olga, of course, beamed radiance as if the morning sun had come out especially for her client. Sasha and Angie's efforts were more likely to terrify children and small dogs but, true professionals, their Steradented dentures were definitely on show, and four rows of tombstones grimaced from between multi-layers of scarlet lip gloss.

Bertha gasped, Detective Inspector Bruce Wallace Mackay, aka the Comb-over King, had pushed the boat out for the occasion: he was in full Scottish regalia complete with kilt and sporran. His famous bald pate was no more. The Comb-over King was wearing a wig. It must be said, in his defence, it was almost the same colour as his own fringe. But 'almost' and 'exact' are not the same thing. True to his Scottish ancestry the shade of deep ginger had been noted and enhanced by the wig maker.

'Oh, my lord,' whispered Bertha, 'pretend you haven't noticed.'

'He looks like a ginger tom,' sniggered Angie, turning her back away from the approaching footsteps. Sasha was shaking with uncontainable mirth. Only Olga stepped forward with an outstretched gloved hand as she realised the white carnation Mackay was sporting could only mean one thing. The Inspector, and not her darling Philip, had bought her services for the occasion. Her expression was as blank as a waxwork doll.

'Ladies! Nice day for it?' the rug-wearer said, rubbing his hands in glee. 'Shall we go in Olga? You look lovely enough to eat.'

A shudder passed through her shoulders, which Mackay put down to the cold breeze, as her hand lightly touched his arm.

'Hang on a bit,' bellowed Bertha. 'Here comes the other two ... ,' she was going to say 'punters', but changed her mind and added 'gentlemen.'

She was right. Both carrying cameras, Philip Bonnay and Chris Cross from the local paper were jostling through the crowd. Both wearing pink and red carnations as instructed by Vera and both obviously expecting to go into church with Olga on their arm.

'Eh, what's all this?' said Philip, grabbing hold of Mackay by the lapel. 'Olga's with me.'

Cross butted in, 'I don't think so sunshine! I ordered the pretty one, not the baggage train.'

'Wot d'you mean by that?' snarled Sasha, handbag at the ready. 'You're no oil painting. Warty!'

Cross had always been self-conscious about the moles on his nose, and the chance remark caught him unprepared with a witty retort.

Philip took the distraction as an opportunity. 'I'll only tell you once. Get your hand off my girlfriend,' and as Mackay did so a stray gust of wind chuckled and caught the marmalade toupee, tugged at the sticky strip securing it to his scalp and lifted it skywards. Mortified as the rug scampered down the steps and bounced across the graveyard in a series of swirls, a bit like a skipping squirrel in Bertha's opinion, Mackay loosed Olga's arm and fled after the escaping pelt, skirt pleats all a-flounce.

Philip tore off the offending carnation and, grabbing Olga by the elbow, scurried her inside to find a seat.

'Come on, then,' said Angie, who didn't have Sasha's aversion to facial disfigurement, pulling Chris Cross by the hem of his jacket. 'Let's make the best of it, dearie. You can't win them all. It could be worse. You could be wearing a skirt and covering your bonce up with a rug.'

Cross, staring down at dumpy little Angie's blinking lashes and ample charms, displayed so prominently by the straps and ruffles, had to agree things could have been worse. There are worse endeavours than spending a couple of hours as the proud hirer of an escort of Angie's vast experience. And, as she patted his behind good-naturedly with be-ringed scarlet-painted fingers, a wide grin found itself spreading all over his face.

By this time Mackay had retrieved the wayward hairpiece from the drain it had landed in, and was squeezing out mud and leaves from over by the lych-gate, watched from a great height by the statuesque Sasha, who was still waiting, with Bertha, by the studded doors. They had been joined by William Warmer, the vicar, who was all of a dither and clearly not himself. Happily, Mackay was unaware of the video camera in the bushes, awaiting the bride's entrance.

'Come on, Inspector. Special offer: two for the price of one,' called out Bertha's booming tones, gesturing for him to take each of them in, one on either arm. As he couldn't find an ounce more mortification in his soul than he had already experienced, Inspector Mackay did as he was bid and took the notorious madam, and sidekick Sasha, down the aisle, unaware that the sodden hairpiece was making a wet patch in his sporran, where in his panic he had hastily stuffed it, and that a trickle of dirty water was slowly dribbling down his leg.

In a gesture of true human kindness Bertha yanked off the sticky strip from his scalp as they took their seats. Fortunately, the scream of agony that ensued was drowned out as the organist struck up, the bridal entrance march . . . 'We All Live in a Yellow Submarine'.

But it wasn't the bride, was it?   EH

Early arrivals for the wedding were knocked out of their various pairs of pinching new shoes as down the aisle shimmied a vision in bright pink on the arm of Royston Montgomery, the golf club pro and an ex-mate of the groom.

There was a collective in-drawing of breath followed by a soft release to a subdued murmur. Who was it in the figure-hugging lycra and jangling jewellery that bounced up and down like newly minted coins on two bags of blancmange? They were shown into seats on Chummy's side in an atmosphere of disbelief.

The bride hadn't yet arrived when Chummy dared to turn around to see who was sitting behind him. He couldn't believe his eyes and dug his elbow into Tom's ribs.

'Ouch.' No best man needs that to add to his shredded nerves. 'Chuffing hell! Chummy, what's up?' He gasped, grinning hard to hide his jitters.

Out of the corner of his mouth Chummy whispered, 'It's her. You know, Joanie Gutteridge from over the railway bridge. She must have won the lottery by the looks of her,' and he all but collapsed on his seat.

Then the swelling notes of the organ announced the arrival of the bride and her bridesmaids and the opening bars of 'We All Live in a Yellow Submarine', rang out once again.

To wed or not to wed   SC

The Church of the Bleeding Heart looked like a rainbow: it was filled with ladies in dresses and hats of every shade and hue. The men looked resplendent in smart suits, and there was even one kilt. Sasha had dropped her bag in front of Inspector Mackay three times but was as yet unable to ascertain if what they said was true.

The Reverend Willie Warmer stood in front of the altar, his vestments newly washed and ironed. The bridegroom, Chummy, stood at the first pew looking very nervous, his best man Tom was trying to calm him down by whistling through his teeth. This only had the effect of making him more anxious. Chummy glanced around him wondering how long they would have to wait for Yvonne, she was always late. Sitting two rows behind him he saw a familiar face, he had to do a double take, to make sure his eyes were not deceiving him. No, it was definitely Joanie, seven years ago she had been the love of his life. Then she had just disappeared, he never knew why. He wondered what she was doing here, then realised he was staring too hard and looked away.

At that moment the door opened and the organ thundered out 'We All Live in a Yellow Submarine', their special song. In walked the two bridesmaids, Ruby and Rosy with small baskets. They smiled broadly as they scattered rose petals in front of the bride. Yvonne's new dress was a billowing tent of white chiffon; they had to cut her out of her original one. Her father, Jim, was walking her proudly down

Willie's Titania aspirations come into view

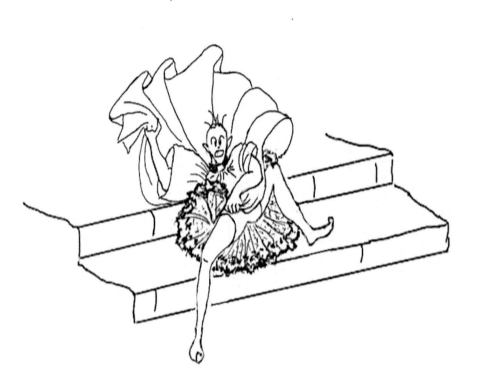

. . . and ended up sprawling with his vestments over his head. There was a gasp from the congregation: all saw their vicar was dressed in a large pink fairy outfit.

the aisle in his full council regalia, his chain of office jingled slightly as they walked.

Diana Ross (not *the* Diana Ross) gazed at her girls with a lump in her throat. She wasn't the only one looking at them, Joanie was staring at them memorised. There was something about the way they walked, the tilt of their heads, the colour of their hair. Her eyes filled with tears, then she screamed and sat down sobbing loudly. All eyes were now on her. The wedding procession had stopped. Yvonne realising she was no longer the centre of attention tried screaming herself, but she was ignored. All eyes were firmly fixed on the distraught figure of Joanie. Royston was trying to comfort her, as he did so, she managed to mumble a few words in his ear in between tears. He stood up and began to speak, 'Sorry about this everyone, but whose children are these charming bridesmaids?' Diana stood up to claim parentage. Royston continued speaking, 'If you don't mind could you tell me a few things? Are you their natural mother?'

'These girls are my life,' she replied, 'but no I'm not their natural mother. We adopted them as babies.'

'Ah, I see.' As he spoke Joanie lifted her head and stared at the twins, tears still streaming down her face, 'Could I ask their birthday and at which hospital they were born?'

'I don't see what business it is of yours, but they were born at the general on the twenty-ninth of April.' At this, Joanie screamed again. Chummy was standing staring at the two women, then he began to count on his fingers. He went very white, as he walked forward to the twins. Yvonne thought he was coming to her and went to faint, he ignored her; he only had eyes for the two little girls. He gently lifted a golden ginger curl and let it run through his fingers. 'Just like Mum's,' he muttered under his breath. He looked at Joanie and asked the question he had wanted to ask her for seven years, 'Why did you go away? I looked for you but couldn't find you?'

Joanie looked at him then turned and pointed, 'Ask him,' was all she said. The whole congregation gasped and stared in the direction she was pointing.

'Dad!' said Chummy, 'What does this mean?'

Sir Lancelot turned very red and flustered, 'Well, my boy, time and place for everything, we can have a long talk about it all later in private.' The congregation groaned as one and shuffled forwards in the pews so they would not miss anything.

'No, Dad, now. Tell me, what have you done?'

There was a cheer from the pews and all eyes were again on Sir Lancelot. 'You were so young. Couldn't have the family dishonoured. She was not right for you. I had my reasons.'

'What possible reason could you have for interfering in my life?'

'I found out something,' Sir Lancelot blustered, 'She, this girl is your ... You just could not be together.'

'No, I don't understand, tell me. I have a right to know.' Chummy started to walk towards his father. Joanie stood and, through her tear-stained face said, 'What he should tell you, but is too much of a coward to, is that I ...'

Sir Lancelot interrupted, 'Be quiet, girl, haven't I

paid you enough to keep silent?'

'I will be quiet no more. We could not be together ... because ... I am your half-sister. It broke my heart to leave you, and give our girls up for adoption, but I had no choice.'

At this Lady Britney jumped up, her very large handbag at the ready, and turned to confront her husband, 'How could you Larry, how could you? When the press get hold of this we'll be ruined.'

All this time Willy Warmer had been standing by the altar. Now as things were getting heated he thought he should intervene, but as he came down the steps he tripped over Gwen, the cleaner, who was still polishing the steps. He rolled down the last three and ended up sprawling with his vestments over his head. There was a gasp from the congregation: all saw their vicar in a large, pink fairy outfit. One or two began to laugh, others tried to stop them. It didn't take long before everyone was shouting at each other, including Bertha, old quarrels and grievances being aired. Sasha took the opportunity to pretend to faint and when she stood up she had a large smile on her face, now she knew the secret of the Inspector's kilt.

While all this was going on, Chummy got near enough to his father: he picked up one of the flower arrangements, which strangely looked like a letter U, and made his father wear it.

Yvonne looked at the mêlée going on around her, and realised she was not going to get married. She couldn't marry Chummy now, not when her brides-maids were his illegitimate daughters by his half-sister, and the vicar was a fairy wannabe. Her own family were bad enough, she didn't want to be saddled with this lot for the rest of her life. She turned to try and leave but everywhere was blocked with shouting people, and flower cushions being thrown around. Then someone whispered in her ear, 'Need a hand, doll, let me be your knight in shining armour.'

She turned to see who it was, and her breath was taken away by the handsome face before her, 'Name's Wytch,' he drawled, 'from the good old US of A.'

'Just get me out of here,' she said, 'I need to be somewhere else. Don't want my whole day to be ruined.'

With that W3 gathered Vonnie up in his arms and strode out of the church just as the bells began to chime, for the wedding that never happened.

Every wedding needs a punch-up   SMS

Overwhelmed by the enormity of the revelations, and after the blushing bride had gathered up a nest of meringue skirts and fled up the aisle followed by the handsome American, a stunned silence descended on the congregation. This deafening hush was broken only by the theatrical sobbing of the groom's step-mother, Lady Britney.

And, of course, if her darling daughter was upset, so was Big Bertha.

'You steaming great heap of vileness,' bellowed Bertha, on her feet with fury spilling forth, the deafening wail blasting forth right next to Inspector Mackay's left ear. 'There's places for men like you, taking advantage of little girls.' Just which heap of vileness she was referring to was up for grabs.

'Belt up, Bertha Snellgrove,' uttered a strident voice behind her. 'Who're you to talk about moral values?' It was Grandma Gutteridge, Joanie's grandmother, wading into the fray. 'We don't need a lesson in morality from the biggest madam this side of Cannock.'

For a big woman, Bertha was light on her pins when she needed to be.

'Might have guessed you'd have crawled out from under the woodwork for a free booze up, Gertie Gutteridge. Come to gloat, have you? Why couldn't you have kept Lady Muck's trap shut? Weren't you lot paid off enough?'

There was a communal gasp.

'Paid off?' snapped Lady Britney, glaring at her nearest and dearest.

At this, Lancelot Fortesque-Chumleigh's knees went, and he sank on to the nearest pew his head in his hands: the newspapers were here, weren't they? Already that mongrel cur, Christopher Cross, and the youngster from the *Evening News* were snapping away with glee, not to mention that gormless lad with his mouth open, who was duly recording the whole event on a video camera for posterity.

Wails of protest were going up from the ginger-haired twins, who were being dragged up the aisle by their outraged mother, while the bouncing bomb-shell, Joanie, their natural mother, was attempting to block their departure with outstretched arms. Fortunately, their stereo screams were being drowned out by Mrs Penrose, the organist, who was very deaf and obscured from view by the organ screen, and who had decided the proceedings must by now be ready for a sparkling rendition of 'Onward Christian Soldiers'. The spirit was upon her, aided by a flask of G&T, and Mrs P was hell-bent: pedal to the metal!

Feeling rather overcome, it was at this moment William Warner took the opportunity to sample the communion wine. Unfortunately, the Vicar forgot Gwen's zealously polished altar steps, and landed base over apex, the incongruous sight of his scanty fairy-suit being displayed to all as the flowing surplus wrapped itself around his ears seeming par for the course.

Ignoring the vicar's predicament and seeing her mother with handbag at the ready, Lady Britney dried up smudged tears and seized the opportunity to have a few quiet words with Chummy over his proclivity for bed-hopping. She was emphasising displeasure with the floral bouquet, which she had been proudly nursing for Vonnie before the bride's abrupt departure. Who'd have thought roses could deliver such a wallop. Tarquine would have been horrified, thought Gwen staring aghast at the mess of petals.

Bums aloft, skirts riding high and stockings sagging, Angie and Sasha made short work of climbing over the back of their pew in a vain attempt to restrict Bertha from engaging in mortal combat with the cause of this catastrophe, the aforementioned Gertie Gutteridge.

'Vhat's going on? Who iz she?' asked Olga of Gwen who was now hovering with the hoover in the nave.

'That's Grandma Gertie, who it must be said, does have a large stake in the ruination of the nuptial festivities.'

'But vhy?' pressed Olga who was totally bewildered.

'On account of Gertie being the great-grandmother of the adopted bridesmaids and mother of the groom's first love and one-time mistress of the father of the groom, who was the father of said first love's daughter, Joanie, and thus grandpa to the curly-tops, which also makes Chummy and Joanie closely related and their resulting offspring ... well, let's just say it was a tightly-knit family.'

Gwen always did have such a nice turn of phrase.

As Angie steered Bertha away from the clutches of Mrs G, and threw a now de-plumed millinery creation towards her in a gesture of placation, Sasha was seeking out Lady Britney to calm the waters before any real harm was done to his Lordship.

'You watch out, Old Slack Draws,' being a parting shot from Gertie that Bertha was not likely to forget in a hurry. But, for now she was preoccupied by her daughter's foot-stamping howls of protest; an injured party herself, Lady Britney was furious: being outshone by that tarty Joanie Gutteridge was no laughing matter.

'Good lawyer! That's all I need, Ma. Who do you know?' It was inevitable her wandering hubby was in for the old heave-ho. Already life at The Mansions was fading from Lady B's thoughts as she stumbled down the steps in the wake of her departing mother, who was still spitting feathers of indignation, her Buck House earrings windmilling in the breeze, and her hired Albert Hall millinery creation hanging about her shoulders in tattered ruination. Whatever would Madam Mordebt say when Gloria returned it?

Following the Trentby Discreet Escort Services party came the ever-hopeful Inspector Mackay who had taken the opportunity to re-affix his sodden hairpiece, albeit if a little askew.

'Vhy iz the vicar vearing women's clothes under hiz ... ?' asked Olga, as elegant as ever, as she glided outside after Philip Bonnay, without so much as a hair out of place.

'Grand British Tradition!' grinned the reporter taking her arm. 'Vicars always do it for weddings.'

Cousin W3 protects his investment   SMS

'You came in that?' said Yvonne gathering voluminous skirts about her thighs and staring aghast at Archie Cavendish's backside. Archie had chosen that moment to inspect the old coach's carburettor, not for any other reason than he preferred fiddling with engines to personal relationship endeavours.

'Any port in a storm, my dear,' whispered Chummy's cousin W3 pushing the red-faced bride up the steps.

'Eh up! Where're you two off to? Where's the flaming groom?' spluttered Archie, wiping his hands on the thighs of his boiler suit as he mounted the steps.

Man of action, Wychita Wainwright-Wilberforce III, always a man with an eye to the main chance, and at that moment with a keen desire to protect his investment, the half-owner of which was now sitting like an over-puffed marshmallow on the back seat, shoved a tenner into Archie's top pocket, where it wrestled with a sucked pencil and a slide rule.

'For some reason best known to herself, the little lady wants to go to a football match,' breathed the American into Archie's oily eardrum. 'We don't want to disappoint her, do we?'

'Course she does,' grinned Archie, and with a belch of blue exhaust, the charabanc reversed down the one-way street at the side exit of the Church of the Bleeding Heart, with only the one mishap.

Perhaps, on reflection, Inspector Bruce Wallace

Mackay hadn't tucked in the unmarked CID car on the double-yellows as prettily as he might have done, and besides a wing mirror isn't the end of the world.

Ye Olde England   ACW

Meanwhile across town ... as the strains of the old English poem 'Jerusalem' by William Blake, sung by the already beer-fuelled lads making up the supporters of Trentby United, faded away, a trill of bells piqued the curiosity of the United goalie, who then got hit full on by a bladder tied to a stick held aloft by a man in a wide skirt.

'Oi, what's your game?' snarled the thick-set Neanderthal-like local butcher, whose surly bulk guarded goal.

'Neigh, neigh, 'tis fertility wished upon ye,' came the reply, and the two-legged 'horse' was reined away, to more bells ringing from who-knows-what part of this centaur-like hobby-horse.

Then a couple of green dragons snaked up the pitch, roaring and dipping, and running hither and thither, chased by the knight St George, brandishing his trusty sword.

Like a bunch of green pansies, thought the Trentby United manager, Ryton.

But old magic must run deep as one dragon slowed, turned menacingly about, hurled aside and ate the manager's ear.

'Get off, yer silly bugger!' he yelled, but for his pains was thwacked with a bladder and the dragon spake thus: 'Live long and prosper,' but was then strangled by huge builder's paws cutting him off in his prime.

The other dragon came to his accomplice's aid and the first fight of the match had begun. Along came two rows of skipping men, merrily waving beribboned sticks, and sporting an arbour full of foliage all around their bowler-like hats. Their white trousers were lashed about betwixt ankle and knee with many brightly coloured ribbons, and their white shirts ennobled by sashes across their manly chests.

The first man in one row was bowled over by the scrapping dragon, and the following row went down like a set of dominoes. The other row joined in the scrap with the manager and the Trentby United team. The loyal supporters came to give a go also but more hobby-horses came in the cavalry charge. The mêlée, each man for himself in a good old Saxon ring of treachery, then ensued to the cheers from the opposing team, Trentby Rovers, and their supporters, who readily joined in.

No-one knew who was fighting whom. It was just good fun. After a few blows to show willing they all sat in the middle of the field and had a beer.

It was this sight that met the eyes of Archie, cousin W3 and Yvonne as they drove up. Always one for a grand entrance, with a theatrical flourish Archie slammed on the anchors, and collapsed the old bus across the gates to the VIP car-park.

The microphone cackled, shrieked, coughed and spluttered to life to the wail of the bride in full regalia, now splattered from the mud off the churned-up football field that had rained upwards to cover all onlookers. The poor soul strode out from the touch-line to kick off the derby match, and all spectators agreed the mascot tripping her over like that was deeply unfortunate ...

Trentby Theatricals   MH

Rudy Darkness, lead singer with the heavy metal band Death and Sunder, loaded their new sound equipment into a clapped out transit van with the help of Cecil Twonk, his drummer and cousin.

'Hey, Jeff, don't you think this new equipment is a little bit overkill for the Labour Club?' Cecil asked.

'My name is Rudy. After today we leave and go to make our fortunes London ... but, mark my words, the whole of Trentby will remember Death and Sunder forever after our performance this afternoon,' he laughed. In truth he was a bit shattered after lugging army surplus canvas about for his mate, Bert Oldcastle. But, ever true professional, he wasn't going to let on, and the reddies came in handy for petrol.

'What are you planning in that devious mind?'

'I like that, Rudy ... Devious ... Darkness; it has a ring to it.'

'Whatever,' said Cecil, as he picked up another amplifier.

Once the van had been loaded they drove over to the Labour Club, where the steward was cleaning the windows.

'Jeff ... I didn't realise Death and Sunder were playing here for the wedding reception.' He sounded surprised.

'Mate, you will be amazed by our farewell performance.'

'Farewell?'

'Yeah, we're going to London.'

'Cool! I'm sure you'll be a success.'

'Thanks,' Rudy said, and began to empty the van. 'Where shall we set up?'

'I've already cleared an area, but isn't that a lot of equipment for the size of the club?'

'No, it'll make the sound quality better, as I said this farewell performance will be amazing,' he smiled ingratiatingly.

'You know best,' he replied, and resumed his window cleaning.

'Oh, I do,' Rudy said under his breath. By the time they had finished setting up the equipment the other members of the band, Mel Madhouse (Larry O'Leary) and Jake Funk (Gerald Granger), were just arriving.

'The equipment looks awesome, where did you get it?'

'Our new agent in London. He says if we want to gig in the city we need good equipment, and I've some tremendous news. On Monday we've a meeting with a record producer, and if it goes okay we'll get a recording contract.'

'You're winding us up,' shouted Jake.

'I'm not! It's our time next year, we'll be playing all the festivals and arenas. How cool is that?' said Rudy excitedly.

'Great! But, I think it's about time to carry out the sound check and then go through the set for today,' suggested Jake.

'Let's do it, but make sure the sound levels are low during the practice, we can whack it up later when all the guests are here,' said Rudy smiling. 'Heavy metal has to be played loud or else something is lost in the performance.'

The band did their sound checks and played through the set before spending the afternoon in the local pub until 'Show Time'.

Horror of horrors   ACW

Manuel and his cohort of cousins arrived in their minibus, garishly painted with their logo and the flat topped pyramids of their Aztec homeland, as the sun set over the immaculate landscaped lawns of Trentby Golf Course Clubhouse.

They were greeted with, 'Hello, you're the entertainment then for the wedding reception? I'm the caretaker, Jack.'

'Good evening, Jack. My name is Manuel Montezuma and these are my cousins.'

'Evening, all!'

The cousins answered in chorus, 'Good evening, señor.'

'You have use of the summer-house out back of the clubhouse for your changing rooms. Park your van on the hard-standing behind it, please. Thank you.'

'Muchas gracias, amigo,' they all said.

'Er, whatever.'

They drove round the drive to the right and parked up. A huge mottled-green marquee resplendent with pennant flags covered the lawn beyond the stone-flagged terrace behind the clubhouse.

'We'll put up the screens and the theatre curtain on the back wall, by the side of those double patio doors. There's up lighting there from solar garden spotlights at the terrace edges and the backlighting from the bar behind the patio doors to give dim lighting for the proper creepy look,' Manuel told his cousins who agreed the location being right, with a chorus of, 'Si, si, bueno.'

The screens hid the players from view as they came from the summer-house to set out the props for the theatre sketch. Beyond the theatre curtains Manuel placed their A-board by the open patio doors announcing the show began at nine o'clock. Manuel occasionally kept a weather eye out for his audience, who began arriving from the left side of the drive to the back of the clubhouse and going on into the marquee.

'Hey, Manuel', said Ramon, 'can you hear a goat?'

'A goat at a wedding reception in England? No, Ramon, they don't do that here,' he explained as he got on with laying out the stage.

A large horned, shaggy head nosed through the theatre curtains and tried to steal a munch from the straw donkey prop.

'Hey, vamos,' shooed Ramon, 'See, Manuel, a goat.'

'Oh, si. What's it doing here?'

Ryton, Trentby United's manager, parted the curtains, 'Sorry mate, Reggie's a strong blighter. It's me team's mascot, and me van's broke down so we can't get him back to the farm. I'll put him up in the old meadow for tonight.' Then looking about the makeshift stage, he observed, 'Oh, it's just like a Spanish fiesta in here.'

'Yes', said Manuel, 'We're from Mexico.'

'Oh, very nice. Me sister went to Cancún one year. Right, must go. Break a leg, as they say.'

'Thank you.'

As the time of the show approached, Ramon asked, 'Manuel, where's the audience?'

'What?' and peeped out from the closed curtains to see no chairs, no-one anywhere, just voices in the marquee.

'I'll go and try and find this Jim Jones who booked us before I get in costume.' Manuel went out from the stage and into the marquee, asking the first person he came across there, 'Is Jim Jones here, please?

A few slurring voices garbled, 'Oh, he's up on top table, he's the father of bride.'

'Mr Jim Jones, please.'

'Yes, that's me. Are you the entertainment?'

'Yes, we're just about to start if you'll direct your guests to our stage on the back terrace, Mr Jones.'

'Hey, aren't you going to play your music in here? You're the band, aren't you?'

'Band?' queried Manuel, his face a picture of puzzlement.

'Yeah, I booked a Mariachi band like them wandering players at restaurants in Spain. Tooty-fruity hats and maracas ...'

'Oh, are they here, too?'

'No, no. You just said you're them.'

'Er, we're the entertainment, but we're a theatre group called Mari Achoe.'

'You what?' Jim Jones sank his head into his hands as the top table exploded into laughter. Word rippled round the marquee with laughter and such, as 'What's he done?' and 'The silly beggar' ringing around the gathered throng of guests.

Janice Jones turned in resignation to her husband, 'Well, we've paid for them, let's go and watch them play, then,' and announced to everyone, 'Follow me, please, the theatre show is starting.' She followed Manuel out to the stage, accompanied by the guests in various stages of merriment.

Manuel took his leave of the wedding party, adding, 'Hope you enjoy our show,' as he went behind the curtains.

A night devoid of moonlight had fallen, with threatening clouds scudding above and the beginning of a howling wind blowing. The trance music began to play as the first rumble of distant thunder rolled.

The curtains parted to show an Aztec temple hung about with straw animals and strange convoluted carved religious symbols. The men were attired in full Aztec ceremonial dress with great feathered head-dresses. The wailing of the festival was sung in chorus, with the loudest and most richest in garb in their centre, obviously a high priest praying with beseeching arms aloft to what now appeared to be a rain deity.

Lightning out beyond the fields lit up the scene in a bright flash for the briefest moment to reveal at the rear of the stage a man with a bleak and terrified face.

The blooming ex-bride, Yvonne Jones, startled, cried out, 'What's going on?' and was comforted with a protective arm by her mother, who ushered her away into the Clubhouse bar.

Lightning flashed and thunder rolled more distantly as a scream rent the air. The actors all went into raised-arm shrieking prayer, and began to dance, pounding and writhing on the spot, and then moving round the priest, who was earnestly crying out in prayer, and trying to part the clouds.

Reggie the goat bleated and writhed in terror at the back of the marquee, jumping about, straining to loose his tether that was tied to the tent peg. The goat finally managed to pull the stake out of the ground, leaving a canvas sheet of the marquee flapping in the wind, which was now growing in strength. No-one heard this commotion over the loud music and the screams and wails of the play's actors, let alone the thunder claps and lightning bolts.

The wind became stronger and the marquee began to pull against the guy ropes holding it down. On stage, the screaming man was dragged to the temple's central flat-topped stone.

The audience stood in silent, awful anticipation. A great clap of thunder shook the air and forked lightning streaked along, under-lighting the clouds. On a crescendo of the trance music, shrill scream of the doomed man and a great cry, from the high priest held aloft a great knife that flashed like a starburst.

The marquee began to billow like full sail of ships of old before slowly taking flight, a corner or a side at a time, the guests so entranced they could not see the unfolding catastrophe behind.

The goat ran crazed in meaningless circles about the writhing marquee, where a snagged line cut one of his legs. A little blood trickled down and, in his irritation at this, he hurled forward towards the terrace, scattering the guests about as he charged on to the stage where the seasoned herdsmen that the actors were, soon caught him and put him upon the sacrificial stone, now, smeared with drops of its blood.

At that precise moment, the clouds parted and rolled away.

FIRE!   SMS/CMH

Straight from the steppes of St Petersburg a wind gusted into the marquee and overturned a display of decorative candles. Guttering wicks chuckled and threw licks of flame at unsuspecting table decorations. Whooshhh ... and some spilled drinks ignited. Laughing now the blaze was running along dribbles of alcohol and, in seconds, the flames leapt to the gauzy hangings and ran up the rear of the tent. The floating balloon roof decorations - a previously half-printed job lot which Vera had got very cheap, all with Chummy's smiling mush plastered on one side and 'EAT AT SID'S CAFE' on the other - were easily conquered by the firestorm.

'Oh, no!' whispered Bertha fearing her end was in sight, as, like the barrage of the Somme, the three hundred or so hydrogen filled balloons exploded one by one, sending molten plastic shreds down to earth as guests dived for cover under tables.

On one of those engulfed tables was a chocolate fountain. The sticky contraption had been assembled by extremely unskilled labour. In far away Japan it had been lovingly designed to work at 125 volts; this meant nothing to Vera and Gloria. Now plugged into a 240-volt extension socket, the chocolate feature with the gherkin dips was a catastrophe waiting to happen.

With the chocolate on the verge of boiling, the fountain was hovering on the verge of an explosion. All that was needed was a spark!

The heavens laughed and added to the confusion. A bolt of lightning struck the Golf Club flagstaff. All the fuses blew. This 'spark' was larger than was needed, but it did the job nicely.

B-A-N-GGG! ... The element in the Japanese fountain blew apart. Dribbles of boiling chocolate splashed out, raining scalding chocolate drops on everything and everyone still within reach. The sudden darkness was lit only by the pallid flames of the unfortunate bonfire and panic ensued.

'Blimey,' muttered Jim Jones from under the top table as a toothpick-speared gherkin narrowly missed his nose and embedded itself in the abandoned handbag of his rapidly disappearing wife.

'FIRE! FIRE! Dial 999,' was the collective alarm of the suddenly sober wedding guests as they fell over each other and tried to race away; whilst the all-day drinkers in the Clubhouse groped at the windows to see what all the fuss was about.

'Was that meant to happen, old boy?' asked the Captain over the top of his ninth G&T. The club pro was too shocked to reply because the fillings in his back molars were reverberating to what sounded like a car engine exploding, but, was, in fact, the first of the tent masts coming to grief.

The commotion was heaven-sent, for one at least. The Aztec theatre troupe had frozen into a tableau, and Reggie the goat on the sacrificial altar seized the chance and sped off across the lawn, taking with him a vital part of the scenery attached to his lead. This trailing appendage collapsed into the spreading flames and caught fire. The wild-eyed beast with the fiery tail was last seen disappearing towards the A449, for all the world as if the animal had taken on a role in a theatrical production of a more biblical setting.

Being delayed by the traffic congestion, the arrival of the fire brigade took some twenty five minutes, by which time the tent had liberally blanketed the nineteenth hole, the first tee and the car park with swathes of burning canvas, setting fire to a number of expensive Rollers, Jags and Beamers that had been parked closest to the members' entrance. To add to the mayhem the main tent poles had yawed, tottered, and then smashed open the Clubhouse roof which, shedding tiles like confetti, screamed in the wind like a scalded cat as the catastrophe unfolded, along with their attic conversion.

Horrified guests huddled together by the fire's edge to keep warm as they waited for the fire engine, before their eyes yet another wing of the Clubhouse disappeared in a wall of roaring flame.

As the *Trentby Evening News* reported, 'It was a wedding reception with a difference'.

It's an ill wind that blows everybody no good, and Olga, as svelte as ever, sheltering in the arms of Philip Bonnay, her newly acquired fiancé and route to permanent residence, had proven herself to be a worthy reporter's mate by rescuing her intended's camera case from the debacle in the marquee as they fled on hands and knees.

As Chris Cross said later, as he sold on the juicy photos to the national scandal sheets, 'A picture speaks a thousand words.' It turned out to be a busy night in the editorial department of *Trentby Evening News*.

Meanwhile in the Labour Club   SMS

The function room of the Labour Club had an air of the *Marie Celeste* about it. Tables were set. Curtains were drawn. All the lights were on but there was no-body home, except for four musicians gearing up for their first half-hour spot. It wasn't their fault the audience was a no-show.

'This is a rum do, Jeff!' said drummer Cecil, rubbing chalk into his palms. 'The bride's cleared off with some tourist and the groom's over there at the bar drowning his sorrows all on his tod.'

'Not our problem, old son. Not our problem. A gig is a gig. We've had cash up front for this lot and I'm damned if I'm giving it back just 'cause Vonnie Jones's had another tantrum and thrown her toys out of the pram. Always was a 'princess', if you ask me.'

'I remember you and that Vonnie Jones in high school,' grinned Cecil with a wink and a nod.

'Water under the bridge,' muttered Jeff, colouring and plugging his guitar into a mega-blaster amp the size of a Mini Cooper. 'Besides, he's not on his tod, is he? There's good old Tom, and the lovely Annabel, to keep him company, and enough of a spread to feed half of Trentby.'

'Only the French half,' replied Cecil. 'Have you seen what's on the menu? Besides, those kids from college have gone home.'

'Not so much silver service as help-your-selves-service, hey? Cheer up, we won't starve.'

At this acknowledged truth, Cecil spat out a wad of chewing gum, pulled it into two pieces and rammed a piece into each ear. 'You ready then, son?' grinned Cecil, pulling a pair of thick socks over the ear-defenders adorning his curly perm and trying a drum-roll to test if he was sufficiently protected. Rudy

Darkness, Jeff's alter-ego, flicked down his shades, waggled his silver boots and nodded. T W A N G, TWANG-TWANG, T W A N G.

All the glasses and optics behind the bar rattled ominously, and even Chummy, who was three sheets to the wind by this time, noticed. He was not alone in this audio-misery. Agog he batted his eyelids and struggled to turn towards the wall of sound slamming into his frontal lobes, which was a big mistake.

Unfortunately for Chummy, the Labour Club had a reserve generator designed to kick-in should any-thing untoward occur to disrupt the electricity supply – very important if a cup-match was being shown on the big TV. As Death and Sunder struck up the first twanging chords of the heavy metal anthem, 'Tie Me to the Cannon of Your Love, Babe', their debut demo-track, two things happened: every light and socket in the place crackled and fizzed as the mains supply was frazzled, and the stand-by diesel-fuelled genera-tor in the basement flicked into life.

Hands clapped over their eardrums, Tom, who had just emerged from the Gents, and Chummy, dived for safety behind the bar where his childhood playmate, Annabel Lloyd, who was moonlighting as a part-time barmaid, was sheltering wearing the dazed look of the shell-shocked and little else. Annabel's blouse was like barbed wire: it protected the property but didn't restrict the view. Chummy's florid cheeks found a soft landing place between Annabel's two underwired fluffy pillows, and an owner who didn't seem in too much of a hurry to send him packing; thus proving every cloud has a silver lining.

But just as Chummy was cheering up, the chorus broke out with the immortal words, 'Send Me to the Devil with a Smile', the inevitable happened and the generator did just as the lyrics said, blowing its gasket with a hiss and a loud bang.

Not so bad an event on its own really, as all the lights went out and the infernal din was extinguished. All would have been well, apart from semi-terminal deafness in the small unappreciative audience, except that the said sparking generator was unfortunately positioned under the gas central heating boiler ...

Apparently, according to the *Trentby Evening News* the explosion was heard as far away as Lower Penkhull, and put considerable strain on the, already over-stretched, emergency services. That the semi-naked occupants of the Function Room crawled out alive from the wreckage, if somewhat blackened and bemused, was nothing short of a miracle.

Perhaps on this occasion the Devil really did look after his own, mused the band's former agent Ray De Wrong, grinning into his coffee as he read the article later that week.

Balloons   SMS/CMH

Funny how the smallest of things are often later found to have been connected ... thought Vera. Earlier that Saturday at one o'clock exactly, after Bertha's hoo-hah departure from the client-waiting area, Vera recalled, 'Just a minute, our Gloria. I've got to put the burglar lights timer on,' and plugged a rather tatty timer into an adapter in the kettle socket with a, 'There, that's it until tomorrow.'

Silence ruled in the portacabin, except for the slight hiss of hydrogen escaping from an 'almost closed' valve on the hydrogen cylinder. The lighter than air gas gradually displaced the nicotine fumes in the upper part of the hermetically sealed box that, thanks to Vera's habit of blocking off anything that could be a draught, was the portacabin.

At about midnight the timer turned the lamp off, causing a slight spark that ignited the highly-inflammable gas. B-A-N-GGG! ... The explosion blew out the door and all the windows, lifted the roof about a foot before depositing it on the car park, and set fire to the remaining gas in the cylinder.

The cylinder shot about, trailing fire like the rocket it had become and smashed across the car park, de-molishing several parked cars and part of a brick wall, before it swallowed its own fiery tail and ex-ploded.

Alerted by a chance passer-by, the fire brigade ar-rived to find all they could do was extinguish what burning materials were left, and do what clearing up they could. 'A good shout,' said one.

The lone police constable who turned out to the distress call was not complimentary about this remark, but words of admonition suddenly dried on his tongue as everyone was distracted by a red glow fill-ing the night sky from the direction of the Golf Club.

The Epilogue: Turned out nice again ...   SMS

'Well, I go to the foot of our stairs. I say, our Vera, I say. What a palaver, the cheek of it. The flaming cheek. I'm glad I wasn't invited now.'

'It's flaming all right,' agreed Vera, wiggling a morsel of battered cod from under her top set while watching trails of smoke rising into the night sky from the debris of the portacabin two streets away. 'Still, Bertha's not daft, she'll be insured.'

'Perhaps, she'll go up market. She's had her eye on that vacant office suite above Madam Mordebt's establishment, you know.'

'And about time. It'll serve Jim Jones right for not giving her planning consent for Number 27. Cheeky beggar. He'll have the pleasure of Trentby Discreet Escort Services setting up right opposite the Council Chamber!'

Gloria grinned a fishy grin, and was just in time to see Archie Cavendish wave to them both as he turned the corner of the High Street driving an old bus with two well-oiled passengers holding forth on the back seat.

'Tell me I'm dreaming, our Vera.'

'No! That was Vonnie, half-cut, with a bloke who didn't look like that drip Chummy to me.'

'That'll be the loaded American cousin,' said a voice coming out of the chip shop.

'Eh up, our Pat. What's the SP?' asked Vera.

Pat Walker selected a crinkle-cut chip with care. 'So I hear, the bride's done a bunk with a rich Yank on account of the unsavoury and varied relationships of a deeply personal nature indulged in by her prospective father-in-law and that swings-both-ways son of his.'

'Word's out, then?' said Vera. 'Like father like son: screw anything that's not got draws nailed down.'

'Trust you two to know in advance of everybody else,' chuckled Pat, opening the door to the cab. 'Having a ride home then, girls, or what?'

'On the house?' asked Gloria. 'On account as we know all the gory details.'

'When isn't it to you two?' replied Pat, who wasn't opposed to exchange a free ride for a bit of gossip.

'It's a Fare Deal!' came the reply in unison as two ample posteriors wiggled on to the back seat gamely holding on to their chip suppers for dear life.

Acknowledgements:

Graphics:

Original Artwork - Pauline Walden

Paper used does not contain chlorine bleach.

Printed by Bookbinding Direct, Keele ST5 5BG